My Husband's Mistress:

Renaissance Collection

My Husband's Mistress:

Renaissance Collection

Racquel Williams

www.urbanbooks.net

Urban Books, LLC
300 Farmingdale Road, NY-Route 109
Farmingdale, NY 11735

My Husband's Mistress: Renaissance Collection

ISBN 13: 978-1-62286-536-9
ISBN 10: 1-62286-536-7

First Trade Paperback Printing October 2017
Printed in the United States of America

10 9 8 7 6 5 4 3 2 1

*This is a work of fiction. Any references or similarities
to actual events, real people, living or dead, or to real
locales are intended to give the novel a sense of reality.
Any similarity in other names, characters, places, and
incidents is entirely coincidental.*

Distributed by Kensington Publishing Corp.
Submit orders to:
Customer Service
400 Hahn Road
Westminster, MD 21157-4627
Phone: 1-800-733-3000
Fax: 1-800-659-2436

My Husband's Mistress:

Renaissance Collection

By

Racquel Williams

ACKNOWLEDGMENTS

First and foremost, I give all praises to Allah. Without him, none of this would be possible. I am forever grateful and definitely blessed.

To my Mom, Rosa, thank you for being there through everything.

To Carlo, you know words can never explain how much you mean to me. I appreciate you.

To my sister Papaya, thanks for having my back. I love you.

To Chris Lee, thank you for being there through the rough times. I love and appreciate you.

To Danielle Marcus, I am so blessed and grateful that our paths crossed. I look forward to many more years of success and laughter.

To Stacey Thomas and Ebonee Abbey, I appreciate the love and support I get from you ladies. I am forever grateful.

To Ambria Davis, even though you drive me crazy, I love you, LOL.

To Kiera Northington, thank you. You're a great editor and friend.

To Tasha Bynum and Sharlene Smith, thanks for the constant promotion of my work. I appreciate you ladies.

To my readers that have been rocking with me no matter what I'm going through, please know I appreciate y'all. Rhea Wilson, LaTanya Garry, Barbara Morgan,

Acknowledgments

Dawn Jackson, Cherri Johnson, Mary Bishop, Kendra Littleton, JoAnn Hunter-Scott, Toni Futrell, Priscilla Murray, Joyce Dickerson, Nola Brooks, Beverly Onfroy, Erica Taylor, Yvonne Covington, Evelyn Johnson , Johnne Johnson, Akia KiaBoo Porter Dessiree Ellison, Qiana Drennen, Donica James, Cherita Price, Redgirl Pettrie, Jane Pennella, Lisa Borders, Muhammad Alexis Goodwyn, Mellonie Brown, Tonya Tinsley, Pam Williams, Tammy Rosa, Venus Murray, Shann Adams, Nancy Pyram, Tina Simmons, Patricia Charles, Temmiyyia Davidson, Nicki Williams Kenia Michelle, Jenise Brown, Kysha Small, Suprenia Hutchins, MzNicki Ervin, Trina McGuire, Rebecca Rogers, Rita King, Stephanie Wiley, Stacey Phifer Mills, Tera Kinsley-Colman and Kesia Ashworth-Lawrence.

CHAPTER ONE

Destiny Clarke

I'd put over ten years of hard work and dedication into my marriage and I'd be damned if I was going to let one of these lower-level whores mess up my happy home. See, I wasn't your regular stay-at-home wife. I'd busted my ass, working side by side with my husband to get his firm started and I had every intention of reaping the benefits that were to come.

In order to understand how I thought about men and their whorish ways, you had to first understand how it all started. First, let me introduce myself: My sperm and egg donors named me Destiny. I was born in the early eighties, right around when the crack epidemic hit hard. My parents were crack addicts and their sorry behinds didn't want me around, so they gave me up for adoption.

Shit, that was cool with me. My new parents were everything that a child needed—or so I thought. Unfortunately, my mother couldn't conceive so I was their only child. The love I got from her was real. I'd never felt like we weren't blood and to this day, she is still the most beautiful person I knew. My parents weren't wealthy; we were what most people considered "middle class." But, I could honestly say I'd never gone without and for that, I was forever grateful.

My mother was one of those old-fashioned women that stayed at home while the husband worked. My father was a military man and by the time I got older, he was retired with honors. I thought it would be good to have him around full-time, but I was soon proven wrong when his attention turned to me. By this time, I was a teenager with the body of a woman. This must've caught Daddy's eyes because I unwillingly became his personal whore. Every night after Mama went to bed, he'd sneak into my bedroom, cover my mouth with one hand, and get on top of me, sliding his cock into my virgin pussy. I used to cry, but eventually I stopped. I would just lie there and take it until he would pull out and bust all in my face. I remembered the first time that bastard forced his cock into my mouth. I bit it so damn hard that he slapped my face.

"Bitch, if you ever say a word I will kill you," he often warned me.

"Shit, that would be so much better than you fucking me," I snarled.

I thought about suicide, but I didn't want to die. I didn't want to tell Mama out of fear that she wouldn't believe me and that they'd return me to foster care. I dreaded that place, so I kept my mouth shut and he kept on having in-house pussy. The entire time, however, I was planning his murder.

I thought I had it all figured out. Mama went to bed early, as usual; I knew the bastard was going to be in my room shortly. I didn't wait for him to come. Instead, I got up and went to the kitchen to make him and myself a cup of tea. I walked over to the den where he spent most of his time. He looked up and smiled as he saw me approach.

"Hey, honey, you look amazing."

I smiled and handed him his cup of tea. I watched as he drank it. I sat across from him with my legs wide open, showing off my fresh young pussy. I knew he couldn't help himself as he started to lick his lips, saliva dripping down his mouth.

He then got up and approached me. My heart raced, but I remained cool. When he tried to touch me, I grabbed his hand.

"No Daddy, you relax. It's my time to show you what I'm made of." I looked at him in a seductive manner.

"That's my baby. I knew you'd eventually see things my way." He grinned wickedly.

I didn't respond. I pushed him on the couch and unbuttoned his pants, releasing his wrinkled, smelly cock. I closed my eyes and started to lick the tip of it. His groans became louder and that motivated me to suck harder. I took his full cock into my mouth and devoured it. About five minutes later, his moans quieted down; I raised my head and saw that the fool had fallen asleep from Mama's sleeping pills that I'd crushed earlier and put in his tea. I got up off my knees and wiped my mouth. I pulled out the big butcher knife that I'd taken out of the cabinet earlier and stood over him. I put it to his chest, but I couldn't bring myself to do it. Tears filled my eyes as I turned to leave, but rage developed inside of me. I turned back around, grabbed his cock and made a clean cut. He woke up screaming bloody murder as he lunged toward me.

"You little bitch! Come here, I'm going to kill you!" he yelled.

I dropped the lifeless cock on the rug and ran as fast as I could. Mama heard the commotion and came out.

I locked myself in my room until I heard the police banging on my door. I opened it, still shaking from seeing all that blood. Deep down, I was happy he was cock-less and that he wouldn't be forcing that shit inside of me anymore.

The police questioned me. That was when I broke down and told them about how Daddy had been fucking me for years. I was only twelve years old and had no charges brought against me because Mama surprised everyone and backed up my story. The authorities ordered me to undergo mental health counseling, however. I heard they were not able to put his cock back into place, so it was safe to say that that bastard wouldn't be fucking another helpless child.

Mama divorced him and we moved from White Plains to Mount Vernon, a neighboring city.

I graduated from high school and went on to nursing school, eventually getting my license as a registered nurse.

My life as a woman would never be the same and men would soon realize that I, Destiny Clarke, was not to be fucked with. Welcome to my world, where you will respect me or get the hell out.

Hassan Clarke

Man, I wasn't goin' lie—ever since I was born, I'd felt like I was God's blessing to these bitches. I wasn't conceited or nothing like that, but I had the looks, my tongue game was fire, and God blessed me with a big dick that most women would kill for. I learned early on from my pops that if you eat that pussy up and lay the dick on her, she would appreciate you and do whatever it is that you wanted her to do. I watched as Mama washed, cooked, and cleaned the house every day and all Pops had to do was fuck her good. I knew that when I grew up I wanted to be just like my pops.

I'd always kept a bad bitch by my side. Don't get me wrong when I say bad: she had to have her own place and her own damn money. I wasn't into the business of tricking on no ho. My dick game was so mean, these bitches always had to pay me to come over and fuck them.

See, I wasn't no bum-ass nigga, I kept a job. I knew that I had to have a backup plan, just in case one of these bitches got to tripping. I was happy when I landed the job at the hospital. Shit, a year earlier I had taken a certified nursing assistant class and got my certification. I didn't mind cleaning up after a mutha-fucka because my goal was to save up enough money to pay for law school. Yes, you heard right—law school. I'd always had a mouthpiece that could get me out of any situation. Mama always said I would make a great lawyer. I agreed because I done talked myself out of many sticky situations before, especially when I got caught cheating.

I was tired of fucking the bitches around the way. Don't get me wrong, these hood bitches kept a wet pussy and had a mean head game. Shit, most of the bitches I fucked with could cook up a good meal, the kind of meals that kept a nigga coming back for more. But all that shit wasn't enough.; I wanted more. Matter of fact, I wanted a "professional woman." The ones that owned their home, drove a nice car, and had a degree in some kind of shit. Yes, that was my definition of a bad bitch. I didn't even care if she had good pussy or not. I had some hood bitches with that wet-wet.

God must've been listening to me because as soon as I started working at the hospital, I laid eyes on one of the nurses. Man, bad little bitch. Nice shape, fat ass, and cute face. At first, I kind of blew it off. I thought there was no way I could pull this one off. That feeling soon disappeared and I was back to my usual self.

I started slowly. I didn't want to seem too thirsty. I gave her little nods here and there. I smiled at her and was always polite. I was reeling her in before I went in for the kill. At first this bitch behaved like she was too good for this kid, but I paid it no mind. I knew it was only a matter of time before I got up in them panties.

CHAPTER TWO

Destiny Clarke

I met Hassan when I was working at Westchester Medical Center as a registered nurse. He was a nurse's aide on the floor that I worked on. He was a handsome brother, but definitely not the type I would've dated. Nothing stood out about him to me; besides, his occupation was to clean shit. This meant he got about ten dollars an hour—pocket change that could barely buy one of my purses. My pussy was high maintenance, so he needed more than that little job to keep me satisfied. I worked every day to make sure I maintained a certain lifestyle, so I wasn't a gold digger, but I wasn't a fool, either. I wanted a man with a big cock and some damn money in his pocket.

Nevertheless, I could tell he was flirting with me, always complimenting me on my looks. I remained polite, making sure I never crossed that line with him. But he was persistent and I had an idea that this fool wasn't going to give up anytime soon.

One day, while walking to my car, I heard some fool hollering my name. I turned around and saw it was Hassan.

"Ms. Destiny, hold on a minute. Lemme rap with you real quick." He jogged toward me.

I stopped in my tracks and mumbled under my breath, "What the fuck does this fool want?" I wanted to get the hell home after working a twelve-hour shift. My damn feet were killing me and I was not in no mood to entertain a man.

"How may I help you?" I tried to sound polite.

"Ms. Destiny, you know I've been feeling you. You know, you are everything that a man could ever want in a woman." He grinned, displaying his set of pearly whites.

I placed my hand on my hip and gave him a look that said, "Cut the bullshit out. What the fuck you really want?"

"You just goin' stand there and not respond? Dang, give a brother a break."

"Hassan, how old are you?"

"I'm twenty-four, but I'm a grown man."

"I bet you are, but I'm not looking for a man. Furthermore, you're still a baby and I am no damn babysitter. You know what I mean?" I said and proceeded to walk off.

"Damn. That was harsh. You must've been with the wrong kind of man. I am a different breed. Trust me. You'll see. I promise, I'm going to show you."

"Yeah, yeah, whatever. I don't have a man nor am I looking for one. I am fine just by myself."

"Damn Ma, I just want to take you out on one date. If you don't like it, then I'll leave you alone. I promise." He looked at me with his big brown eyes.

I felt something inside of me shiver. I wasn't looking for a relationship, and definitely not with a boy, but here he was, asking me for a date. *Shit—I might as well*, I thought. I was tired of always being alone in the house. I was a workaholic and when I wasn't at the hospital, I was home. Every other weekend my childhood girlfriend Amiya and I would usually go out for dinner and drinks. That summed it up for my personal life. I hadn't had any cock in a while and I was getting tired of fucking myself.

"All right, we can go on one date. But trust me, if you step out of line, I will fuck you up. You hear me?" I warned.

"Hold up! It's only a date. You behaving like we about to get hitched or something," he said, and we busted out laughing.

We exchanged numbers and scheduled the date for the following weekend, my day off. He walked off in full speed like he'd just hit the jackpot.

I shook my head as I walked off, entered my Chrysler 300, and drove off. I smiled to myself, *I see I still have it*, I thought. Boy, this little nigga didn't know what I had in store for him.

Our date night was approaching and since I hadn't been around a man in the past year, I was a little excited. I couldn't lie—I missed getting fucked on the regular, but I preferred to fuck myself, rather than settle for these low, lying-ass men running around NY. I deserved to be treated as a queen.

I heard my phone ringing while I was cleaning up. Hassan was on the line when I picked up.

"Hello Hassan, how are you?"

"Hello Ms. Destiny. I just wanted to know if you could pick me up?"

"Huh?" I asked to make sure I heard right.

"My cousin was supposed to give me a ride to the diner, but he cancelled at the last minute. I hope you don't mind."

"No, I don't mind. Give me your address." I took the address and hung up the phone.

I lied. I did mind. This nigga didn't have a car. What the fuck! I wondered if he lived with his mama too. Oh hell no, he definitely was not my kind of man. I wasn't a taxi service and I won't be driving this fool around. I should've cancelled our date, but something about him seemed intriguing.

I drove to Fourth Street to pick him up. I was shocked to see him walk out of a house with the paint almost gone on the outside and that appeared to be abandoned. I watched as he walked toward the car. He had cleaned up pretty well. I guess he was trying to impress me and it paid off because when he got in the car and sat down, I wanted to reach over and tongue him down. I was a lady however, so I contained myself.

Our first date went well. I thought I'd have to pay for our meal, but he covered it. He was also a gentleman, opening the car door for me and everything. These were small things, but they meant a lot to me.

I pulled up in front of his building and stopped. I noticed he sat there, looking at me.

"Well, thanks for dinner. I really enjoyed myself. You are pretty cool."

"So this is it? The night is still young. Come up. Let's watch a movie or something."

My mind was telling me no, but my heart was telling me yes. I had to admit it; my pussy was begging to go.

"All right, let me park, but you better not be on no slick shit."

"Man, don't do that. I'm a standup dude. If you ain't giving me the pussy, I don't want it."

"Mm hmm," I said, and got out of the car.

I was nervous going up in his apartment, but I had my mace on my keychain, so I was ready in case anything happened.

He lived in a small one-bedroom apartment, but you could tell that he was a neat freak because nothing was out of place—you know my nosey ass was paying attention to everything. He poured me a glass of cheap wine and took out a Heineken for himself. We sat on the couch in the living room, talking about all kind of things. He kept pouring wine and I kept drinking. It didn't take long for me to start feeling the buzz. I felt good, so I lay across the couch and placed my legs on him.

"Come here," he pulled me up toward him.

"Why, what you doing?"

"Nothing, just want you close to me."

"Boy, this our first date."

"So what, we're grown. There are no special rules."

I didn't fight it. Truth was I loved the feeling. He picked me up and took me to his bedroom. He stood me up, even though I could barely stand on my feet. He went up under my dress and unsnapped my bra, dropping it to the ground. His hands sent an electric sensation through my body as they ran down and removed my panties. I was flooding with a year of backed-up pussy juice. I put his finger in my passion hole and afterward he put it to his lips and licked it clean. Honestly, all I could think of was his cock entering me. Instead, he got on his knees, spread my legs, and started licking my pussy from the back to the front. I held on tight to the bedpost and the wall as I groaned out in ecstasy. It was the best feeling ever and I wanted to yell as he dug his tongue into my hole. I screamed louder, wanting him to fuck me.

"Do you like it, baby?"

"Yes, I love it, please fuck me," I pleaded.

He didn't pay me any mind. Instead, he placed my legs above his shoulder and sucked harder on my clit, holding it hostage for a while. I couldn't contain myself; I had multiple orgasms as I released all the backed-up cum that was inside of me. I was ready to get fucked, but he didn't seem to want to. He let me down and placed me back on the bed.

"What the fuck, you don't want this pussy?"

"I do, but not yet. Tonight was just a little something to let you know I'm feeling you. I'm trying to make you my woman. Straight up."

"I understand that, but my pussy is on fire. You going to leave me hanging?" I asked.

"Destiny, I would love to fuck you, but I want more from you. See, I could get pussy on the regular, but you're so much more than a fuck. I want you, woman."

I guessed I should be happy that his ass respected me so much, but I was a little irritated. I felt stupid that I was begging the nigga and he turned me down. I managed to stand up and grabbed my bra and drawers.

"What you doing?"

"I'm going to wash off and then I'm going home."

"No, you're not. You are in no position to drive. Lie down and get some rest."

Damn! This nigga just checked me. Any other time I would've snapped, but this time was different. I loved his in-control attitude. *Maybe this could be something that would be great for me*, I thought. I rolled over on his pillow and inhaled his strong, masculine smell—I fell asleep instantly.

CHAPTER THREE

Destiny Clarke

Things between Hassan and I developed quickly. He finally gave me the dick and I was too gone. See, every man knew how to slide their cock in a hole, but it takes a unique man with skills to serenade a woman physically and mentally. The brother knew how to do that and he ate my pussy like a pro; he even licked my asshole, which sent me into frenzy. I wasn't ashamed to admit that I loved it when he blew in my asshole. Within weeks, I was totally in love with this stallion. The amount of energy he had surprised me; we would fuck for hours at a time without taking breaks and when he busted, it took nothing but a little foreplay to get him hard again. I loved a man that knew what to do with pussy.

We kept our relationship private while we were at work. I wasn't ready to show him off to the world. I wasn't proud that I was fucking the nurse's aide and I damn sure didn't want those bitches at my job to be gossiping behind my back. It was kind of hard at work not to be all up in his face, and I started to feel jealous when the younger nurses or nurse's aides were all up in his face.

Things progressed smoothly. At first, he would be at my place three to four days out of the week, but then it became every night. We talked about it and decided it would be best for him to give up his one bedroom and move in with me. It became easier because I didn't have to chauffeur him back and forth. It also was great for me because I got my pussy eaten every night and I had my own in-house cock. Life was great after all.

The little money he earned at the hospital was not much, but I paid most of the bills and he bought the food. I wasn't really tripping because I knew the situation before I got in it. We ended up having a conversation about what he wanted to do in life, and he informed me that he'd always wanted to go to law school. I think it was a great idea and I was willing to help him through it.

He quit his job at the hospital and enrolled at Columbia University in Manhattan. I bought him a brand new car, a whole new wardrobe, and fixed him up. He was entering the corporate world and needed to dress the part. Yes, you could say I upgraded him. Pretty soon, he was making good grades and his future was looking brighter.

I went to the doctor earlier that day because I wasn't feeling well. Big surprise—I was pregnant with our first child. I was so excited at the thought of having my own children to take care of. I'd made a vow a long time ago to be the best mother I could be. Unlike my donors, I was going to take care of mine. I got home and waited for Hassan to return home from school.

"Hey honey," I greeted him as he entered the door to our house.

"Hey love, no work today?"

"No, I wasn't feeling well so I took the day off and went to the doctor."

"You okay? Why you didn't call me? You know I would've come home."

"No, I didn't want to bother you, but I have some good news for you."

"What honey? Spit it out, you know how I hate surprises."

"We're having a baby!"

"You playing, right?" He seemed surprised.

"No, I went in because I kept having these headaches and feeling nauseated. I thought I had a stomach bug, but the doctor ordered a pregnancy test and I found out I'm pregnant."

He grabbed me and pulled me closer to him.

"Damn, I'm happy as fuck. I'm going to be a father. Hell yeah! We need to make it official, before my seed enters this world."

I blinked twice and looked at him for confirmation.

"Yes, I said we need to get married. We going to be a family."

That took me by surprise, but I had to admit that I had been thinking about it for months; We lived together and we were planning a future, so why not make it legal? I was even more excited to know that he felt the same way about me.

"Oh, I see we have a wedding to plan."

"Yup, you will now wear my last name proudly," he boasted.

"You know I will. I'll become Mrs. Clarke," I joked back.

We sat down, had dinner, and continued talking about parenthood. This would be our first child, so I thought we were both looking forward to parenting.

Hassan Clarke

I felt like I hit the jackpot once I started fucking with Destiny. She wasn't like the other bitches that I had fucked with. She had some aiight pussy, she sucked a mean dick, but it was the money that kept me around. The only issue I had with her was that after I gave her the dick, she got sprung. I didn't trip though, 'cause in no time, I was living at her house. That was only the beginning. After telling her about my dream of going to law school, she surprised me when she told me she'd help me. She bought me a car and a whole new wardrobe. Fuck, I was so damn happy I almost jumped up, but I caught myself. I couldn't risk her knowing that I was only looking for a paid piece of pussy.

I was shocked when she told me she was carrying my seed. Don't get me wrong—I've always wanted kids. I just wasn't ready and I wanted to have kids with the woman that I loved. I was still enjoying my life and didn't want to be tied down or have any baby mama drama.

I saw some of my homeboys going through hell with their children's mother, and they'd be taking out that child support on their asses. I was lost for words when she blurted out she was pregnant. My dumbass was so shocked I blurted out, "Let's get married." I tried to catch the words, but it was too late. I didn't have a choice but to pretend like I meant every word. Destiny was happy and my daddy always told me, "Happy wife means happy life." I hoped that old fool was correct.

In no time we were inseparable, living as a couple. I thought it was cool at first. I swear I tried to be the good man, but the hoes kept calling and my dick was getting antsy. I realized that I was not ready to settle down with one piece of pussy.

We finally tied the knot and started our lives.

I had an issue that I had to deal with. I had this chick that I was still dealing with on and off. She called me over to her house a few days after I got married. I knew she hadn't heard about me getting married because she would've gone the fuck off. God knows that bitch wasn't too right in the dome. I figured she missed me and wanted the dick. I got out of class early so I could stop by her crib. I pulled up feeling like a child in a candy store.

I walked over to her apartment and pushed the door. It wasn't locked because she was expecting me. I entered the apartment and saw her seated on the sofa. The sight that was in front of me was enough to make me bust, before I entered the pussy. I had to give it to her—she was a bad bitch with a phat pussy and she could suck a nigga dick dry. At one point, I thought about wife-ing her ass, but I just couldn't bring myself to commit. I liked it the way it was set up. I did me and she waited until I came around to fuck her. Imani wasn't a fool. She knew she was the only bitch that I would spend a dollar on if I ever decided to settle down on the real. She would be my only woman.

I didn't bother to say a word; I took off my clothes and knelt down. The sight of her juicy pussy was driving me insane. I dug my face into it and started to tear it apart. You would've thought that I was famished from the way I was going in. But, that wasn't the case; the pussy was just good as fuck. You had to be a nigga to understand what I was feeling.

"Daddy, oh, this feels so fucking good."

"Bitch, shut up and spread your legs."

"I love it when you talk dirty to me, Daddy," she mumbled.

Her moans were enough for me to flip her over and ram my dick into her ass. She was a pro when it came down to getting fucked in the ass. She handled that dick like her ass was hungry, which made me go in even harder.

"Take this dick, bitch. Take it!"

"*Awww*, Daddy, give it to me. I love you, Daddy. I love you." Her words sounded like a sweet melody.

"I love you too, baby girl, now take this dick."

Within minutes of busting in her ass, she sucked me off and my dick was rock hard again. I entered her wet pussy and put her feet over my shoulder. Her pussy was so tight that it gripped my dick with force. I beat those walls up, totally ignoring her cries. About fifteen minutes later, I nut all in her pussy, and it was a decision that I would soon regret.

I leaned back on the sofa and watched as she walked into the bathroom. I whispered a silent prayer, hoping her ass was on the pill. I damn sure didn't want a baby in the equation right now, especially when Destiny was already carrying my child. My thoughts were interrupted when she entered the room.

"Damn boo. You laid the pipe down this time. I feel like you've been practicing. I hope you're not fucking nobody else."

"Don't come at me with no bullshit. I've always fucked you good. And why the fuck are you worrying about who I'm fucking?"

"Damn! I was only playing with you. I ain't worried about no bitch as long as you keeping me happy, Daddy."

This bitch didn't know it, but she just blew me. One thing I hated was a jealous-ass female. Shit, to me, these hoes were stingy. Trust me—I had enough dick to go around evenly. Ain't no need to be greedy.

I gathered my clothing, went into the bathroom, and got into the shower. I washed thoroughly so I could remove any scent of another woman. I couldn't risk Destiny smelling sex or even the mere smell of another woman. I got out, dried off, and got dressed.

I kissed Imani on the forehead and left, turning on my phone as I walked to my car. I glanced at the time and realized it was late as fuck. I knew Destiny was wondering where the fuck I was. My mind went into overdrive. I had to come up with the perfect reason as to why I was just making it home this time of night.

By the time I pulled up, I had the perfect story in my head. I was a little tired, but I had no intention of going to bed before I made love to my in-house bitch. I had to shut her up one way or another and a good fuck always did the trick.

CHAPTER FOUR

Imani Gibson

Okay, here we go again. I was tired of this nigga Hassan playing games with me. I mean, I'd been messing with his ass since he was doing his CNA classes on White Plains Road. His sister Charmaine was my best friend. That's how I knew every time when he was playing games with me. She had no problem letting me know that nigga was no good for me. Trust, I didn't need her to tell me. I knew that he was fucking other bitches.

It was cool with me at first because I was also fucking other niggas. I even fucked his homeboy, Corey. Hassan's ass was cool at first, but the minute I gave Corey the pussy, Hassan got real disrespectful. He started calling me a bitch and a ho when he couldn't get his way. I wasn't used to fucking with a broke-ass nigga, but the way that nigga ate my pussy and fucked me good, I was sprung on the dick. I tried to fight my feelings for him, but I couldn't. I quit fucking all the other niggas I was fucking around with and tried to stay true to him.

Yes, I believed all his lies. He spoke about marrying me and moving me out of the projects. I knew he didn't have any money at the time, but his hustle was crazy; somehow, he always managed to get money. He was the only man that ever looked out for me the way he did, so I remained true to him.

***

"Bitch, what's going on wit' you? Haven't heard from you in a minute," Charmaine asked me over the phone.

"Nothing, just laying low. You know yo' brother don't want me outside around these other niggas," I proudly said.

"You a fucking fool if you listening to his ass. He out there around other bitches."

"I know you mean well, but I love yo' brother. I mean, I want a future wit' him, so I ain't goin' to fuck up what we got going on for these ole broke-ass niggas," I spat.

"Bitch, do you, but you loyal to a nigga that don't give a fuck 'bout you."

"Damn Charmaine! Why you got to be so negative? I mean, can't you be happy for me and him?"

"Listen, you're my fucking friend and I don't like the way he treats you. Furthermore, did that nigga tell you he got married?"

I paused. I wasn't sure I heard her right. I knew she didn't want us together, but I never imagined her going this far.

"Girl, quit playing. The only person your brother gonna marry is me. We might have our problems and all, but we're working them out."

"You ain't got to believe me. Call Ma and ask her. Better yet, the next time you see that nigga, ask him to see his phone and look up Destiny in there. You better wake the fuck up and stop being a piece of ass to a nigga that barely gives two fucks about you. You're too pretty to settle for that."

I was lost for words. I felt tears welling up in my eyes. I didn't want to believe what she was saying, but I knew that she wouldn't lie to me like that.

"Listen, I'll hit you later," I said, and then quickly hung the phone up.

"No!" I screamed out in my apartment.

I loved this nigga and I thought he was feeling me too. I was dead wrong. I had to know the truth.

Just like I thought, that nigga rolled over to the house like nothing happened. I already had a plan in motion. I sat across from him and just gazed at this snake-ass nigga. I couldn't believe that he played me like that. Well I didn't need to indulge in a pity party. I got up and took off my nightgown. I watched as his face lit up and he grabbed me and pulled me toward him. As he fucked me, I threw the pussy on him. I needed him to know that there wasn't another bitch in this life that could fuck him like I did. Shit, I might not have had anything, but I knew I had pussy.

I screamed and moaned louder to get him excited. In no time, he busted all up in my pussy and a few minutes later, he was laid up snoring on my damn couch, like an old hog. I waited for a few minutes to make sure he was really sleeping, then slowly picked up his pants and tiptoed to the bathroom. I took out his phone.

As I scrolled, I saw the name "WIFEY." I proceeded to check the text messages and in front of me was all the proof I needed. I put his phone back in his pants, wiped my eyes, and walked out of the bathroom.

CHAPTER FIVE

Destiny Clarke

I was about three months pregnant when we got married. It wasn't a huge wedding because I didn't have any family besides Mama. My best friend and my co-workers also came. Hassan's family was present. He came from a large family of women. I didn't really click with females and I was not going to get cozy with my in-laws. I knew how it worked—as long as things were fine with the man, they'd love you, but the second you decided to kick his behind to the curb, they'd all turn against you. I've had my share of bad luck with in-laws before, so I kept my distance. The wedding was nice. Mama cried and told me how happy she was that I found love. I think after what happened when I was young, she thought I would never be happy. I thought so too; so far, this was the first time I could say that I was happy with my career, my husband, and baby on the way. We decided to honeymoon in the Bahamas after I had the baby; I sure didn't want to go on vacation looking like a whale.

I really thought everything was going well, but weeks after the wedding, I noticed Hassan was coming home later and later. I first dismissed it, thinking that he was leaving school late. That was until one night when that fool didn't make it home until after midnight. I called his phone numerous times and it went straight to voicemail. I thought maybe something bad had happened to him, but I soon rejected that idea. I would've heard if something happened to him. I couldn't sleep, so I lay on the living room couch, watching television and patiently waiting for my husband to come home.

It was five minutes after twelve when he pushed the door open. I sat up on the couch, which startled him, because he didn't expect me to be awake.

"Really, where the hell have you been? I've been calling your phone." I stood up in front of him.

"I was out with a few of my school friends. We drove uptown and were just sitting around kicking it. I didn't even know it was this late. I'm sorry, Babe."

"Really Hassan. You're a fucking married man. You just don't walk up in the house any ole time of night."

"Dang Babe, calm down. I know I'm married, but that don't mean that I have to be locked up in the house all the damn time."

"You're full of shit. Whenever there's smoke, trust me, fire is close behind. I will not be your fool, trust me on that. If you have all this time to hang out, then you can fucking work and help pay some of these damn bills," I said with venom in my voice.

"That was deep. I want to work. Don't you dare accuse me of being lazy. It was your idea for me to go to school full-time."

"Boy, whatever, you're a fucking joke," I said before I walked off into the room.

That was our first quarrel and I was fine with it. Deep down, I had a feeling that he was with another woman. The entire time that we'd been together, he had never up and disappeared without answering his phone. I didn't have any proof, but deep down, my intuition was telling me I was right.

I went days without talking to him. I needed him to know that I was not going to tolerate any kind of disrespect from him, or anyone else, for that matter. He tried to play around with me, but I stopped him dead in his tracks. Once you let a man believe that they can get away with certain things, they will try to the next time around. Hassan didn't know that I only gave a man one chance to fuck up. After that, he'd be in the doghouse just like the rest of the no-good-ass men.

Things eventually returned to normal. He was doing great in law school and I was on maternity leave, so I had some free time on my hands. I noticed there were times when his phone would constantly ring at night. He would look at it, then look at me, and utter, "That's my boy. I done told his ass not to call me this late." I would look at him and smile. That nigga really thought I was a dumb bitch. I wasn't dumb. I was only buying time until I had my baby. Then he'd find out who he was fucking with. I promised on my unborn seed that Daddy was in for a treat if he didn't get his act in order.

CHAPTER SIX

Destiny Clarke

I was weeks away from giving birth to my daughter. I was as big as a house, but I was excited that a little "mini-me" was about to be popped out. I hoped that I could give her all the love her little heart desired. I made a vow to protect her by any means necessary and prayed to God daily that none of these pervert-ass niggas would ever come close enough to breathe on her. I wasn't a killer, but I would damn sure kill to protect mine.

It was a relaxing day for me; I was home alone as usual. Hassan was at school. I didn't expect him to be home any time soon. I heard my phone ringing and I was going to ignore it, but decided not to. I figured it might be my girlfriend calling. She'd been calling every afternoon to check up on me. I couldn't help but love her crazy butt. We'd been friends since high school and had remained close. I grabbed my phone, thinking it was her.

It was a 914 number. I didn't recognize it, but I picked it up anyway.

"Hello."

"Yes, hi, can I speak to Destiny?"

"Speaking, may I ask who's calling?

There was a pause and heavy breathing into the phone.

"Hello, are you still there?"

"Yes, I am. See, you don't know me, but I know of you. I want you to know that we are both fucking the same man."

It was my turn to pause. I was caught off guard with this piece of shit on my line. All kinds of thoughts rushed through my mind, but I took a breath and regrouped quickly.

"So, you're saying you are fucking my husband?"

"Husband? He ain't married. Plus I'm pregnant with his baby."

"Listen to me you little whore, I don't know why you called my phone to tell me my husband is fucking you. I'm pretty sure you ain't the first and won't be the last. Please get in line with the rest of the whores that're waiting to take my place. As far as you being pregnant, I don't give a fuck about you and that illegitimate little monkey. Don't you call my fucking phone again. You hear me, you low life piece of shit?" I didn't wait for a response; I hung my phone up.

I had to sit down on the bed. My head had started to spin. I knew that grimy-ass nigga was fucking around on me, despite all that I did for him. I was so fucking angry that tears began to roll down my face. I had flashbacks of when my daddy used to fuck me and how hurt I used to be. I felt the same fucking way. I trusted this bastard with my fucking life and this was how he repaid me. I lay there and cried for a little while, but I soon dried the damn tears and got up. I was too good of a woman to be crying over this broke-ass nigga. I had to figure out my next move.I took a hot shower, made a cup of tea, and got into bed to watch *Forensic Files*. Its episodes were off the chain. Mama used to watch it, and that was where I got the idea to put the sleeping pills into Daddy's tea. You could learn so many things just by watching television.

I heard the door when he opened it, but I remained upstairs. Then he entered the kitchen. His ass was hungry, but I'd be damned if I was going to cook for this sorry-ass nigga who had been out slinging his dick everywhere, his sidepiece talking 'bout she's pregnant. I'd be a damn fool if I continued to let him use me to pay for his schooling, but all that shit was about to be over.

"Hey Babe, I thought you cooked?"

I sat up in the bed so I could address him the correct way.

"Your whore called my phone today," I said and stared him dead in the eyes.

"Wh. . . Wha. . . What you talking 'bout?"

"You heard what the fuck I said. Your baby mama, aka your whore, called me today to let me know you've been fucking both of us."

"Destiny, cut that shit out. I've no idea who called you. I only have one child on the way and it's with you."

"You are a lying fucker. You can't even lie straight. I can't believe that I picked up your broke ass and brought you in my shit and you have the fucking balls to be out there fucking around on me? You are a sorry excuse for a man. You make my fucking skin crawl," I shouted at him.

"I feel that you're upset, but you need to calm down. You're pregnant and shouldn't be getting all riled up," he said and tried to touch my arm.

I took a step back and slapped his hand away.

"Don't fucking touch me. I'm a fool for believing you. I knew you were out there fucking around all those nights you came in late. Too tired all of a sudden to fuck. No, your ass was too tired from fucking that bitch. Then not only that, your nasty ass didn't even use a condom." I looked at him with disgust written all over my face.

"Destiny, chill out wit' all that. I ain't fuck nobody, since I been with you. You gotta believe me, I don't know who called you, but they need to quit playing."

I couldn't take any more of his lies, so I walked away, down the stairs. I saw straight through his bullshit. I was mad at myself for picking this lame-ass nigga. I just couldn't believe that he played me like that. I thought about cutting his cock off just like I did Daddy's, but that would be too easy. I made me some peppermint tea and lay on my couch. I was not sleeping in the bed with a man that I considered an imposter.

Hassan Clarke

The minute that Destiny said someone called her, I knew who it was. That bitch Imani played too fucking much. I had no idea how she found out that I was married or how the fuck she got Destiny's phone number. I scanned my brain and soon realized it had to be the other day when I stopped by. That bitch fucked me so good, I literally passed out on the bed. I woke up hours later, just to make it home a little before 12:30 a.m. That was the only time her sneaky ass could've gone through my phone.

Even though she caught me off guard, I was still on point. I tried to convince her that I had no idea who she was talking about, but she wasn't tryna hear that shit. I really didn't feel like hearing her mouth, but then again, I couldn't risk her cutting me off. To be honest, I felt like smacking the shit out of her when she came out of her mouth sideways, calling me all those fucking names. This bitch had no idea who the hell she was fucking with.

I stood there as she showed her black ass. It was funny how bitches acted like they were all high and mighty until the minute they got mad. But, I saw that Destiny wasn't any different from the regular hood bitches. She was an educated hood rat bitch, and that made it even worse.I tried to calm her ass down, but she slapped my hand away. That was it for me because I might've snapped and broken that bitch's neck off her body if she touched me. See, Daddy taught me that if she's woman enough to touch you, then she's woman enough to take an ass whooping. Mama never tried him like that, so I understood his logic perfectly.

I was happy when she finally left the room because my blood was boiling and I didn't want to do anything that I was going to regret. I was heated that Imani pulled some shit like that. That bitch was playing a dangerous game, fucking with my meal ticket like that.

I sat on the edge of the bed with my head in my hands, irritated as fuck.

After class, I rushed to the Bronx. I might've run a few stop signs trying to get to Imani's apartment on Gun Hill Road. I ran upstairs to apartment 212-A and banged on the door.

"What a surprise! You didn't tell me you was coming by today."

I pushed her backward and stepped into the apartment, locking the door behind me.

"Bitch, shut up! Why'd the fuck you go through my phone?" I yelled.

"Boy, whatever! Oh, you ova here going off over some bitch. It must be true then; you're fucking married! When the fuck were you going to tell me, huh, nigga?"

"It was none of your business. I'm not your fucking man."

"Nigga, you grimy as fuck. I stayed faithful to your dumb ass. I never fucked another nigga, even when I could. I fuck you and suck you good and this is how you repay me? You went and married the next bitch. I fucking hate yo' ass, for real."

"Whatever, yo! I had to do what I had to do. Shit, I tried to tell you to sell your pussy so we could make some money, but you wasn't tryna hear that. Shit, you knew what I was tryna do, but yet you didn't try to help me. Yet you all up in my face, because the next bitch stepped up to the plate."

"You know what? Fuck you. Me and my baby don't need yo' ass anyways," she spat, venom dripping in her voice.

I looked at her thinking, *Did I hear this bitch right*?

"Bitch, what you mean? You and your baby? Your ass ain't pregnant and if you were, that shit ain't mine. You better find that nigga that you was fucking."

"Boy, please. I'm pregnant. Here go the fucking paper." She grabbed a piece of paper off the table and handed it to me.

"Fuck you! I wasn't fucking anybody else. You just mad that I told yo' fucking wife about our relationship and now you 'bout to be a daddy," she laughed out loud.

I stood there, lost for words. *This can't be real*, I thought. She was playing with me. Maybe she was trying to get some abortion money out of me.

"Man, what the fuck ever. Shit, what you need the money for, the abortion? How much do you need?"

"Get the fuck out of my shit! I don't need your fucking money; I plan on having my fucking baby. Yeah, I know about your love child, so you think I was about to kill my child while you and your bitch enjoy your fucking bastard? You should know me better than that, Daddy." She winked at me.

At that moment everything around me turned black and I stepped toward her. I put my hand around her neck, trying to shake the life out of her. I don't know what made me snap out of it, but when I looked down on her, she was barely breathing. I let her neck go and walked hurriedly out the door. I sped out of the parking lot and headed up White Plains Road. I wasn't sure if she'd called the police and they were out looking for me.

I was hurt and confused as I drove home. I knew I shouldn't have done what I did, but that bitch was making a fool out of me. "A fucking baby," I mumbled. It's bad enough I already had one child on the way, now here this bitch goes, telling me she was knocked up. *I need a fucking drink, bad.* I made a detour and headed to Nereid Avenue. I had to talk to somebody and who better than my homeboy, Mari.

Mari had a few baby mamas, and went through drama on the regular. I used to sit back and laugh at him when he would tell me all these different stories. Now, here I was in a fucked up situation. My gut told me that bitch was lying, but common sense told me she might be knocked up. I recalled the day I busted in her—a damn stupid move on my behalf—a move that might cost me everything.

CHAPTER SEVEN

Destiny Clarke

The day that my daughter arrived was the best day of my life. I now had someone to love and protect. I'll admit, she came out looking just like her daddy, but she had my high cheekbones and my complexion because I was two shades lighter than Hassan was.

He was also excited, or so he seemed. I wasn't buying any of that. I couldn't get it out my head that he had another baby on the way. He kept denying that he knew the bitch or that he had an affair. I knew he was lying. There were a lot questions like, how did this slut get my number, if he wasn't fucking with her? He had all the answers, but he took the coward's way out. What kind of man denies their child? From that day on, I lost all respect for him.

After my baby was born, things changed between us. I hadn't forgiven him for cheating on me, nor did I forget that another bitch was carrying his seed. I just kept my cool because my baby deserved to have her daddy in her life. I didn't know my parents and didn't want my child to go through the same shit.

I know, maybe my thinking was wrong, but fuck, I didn't care about being wrong. My child was going to have both her mommy and daddy in her life. Even if it meant that I was going to suck up the ill will that I have for Hassan's cheating ass and act like we're the perfect family.

The sad thing was that this bastard thought that I had forgotten that bitch had called. There wasn't a day that went by that I didn't think about him fucking her raw and now he had a little bastard on the way. I hope that bitch knew that my daughter came first at all times. I really didn't give a damn if that little bastard was hungry or needed diapers. For one, Hassan's ass was still broke; and two, there's no way in hell my money was going to feed that little monkey. I'm not harsh. That's just the way life is set up. I busted my ass to make sure my baby Amaiya had everything that she needed, so that bitch needed to sell her pussy or suck a few more dicks so she could provide for her monkey.

I waited around to see if he was going to confess about the affair, but that lying-ass bastard kept quiet. I checked his phone a few times, but there were no messages beside mine. He was always on time when he got out of school; no matter how I tried to catch him in a lie, he never slipped up. Either he wasn't cheating or he was a pro at cheating and knew damn well how to cover up his tracks.

"Baby, you know ever since you came into my life, it's been so much better."

"Really? Which part is better? Is it the part where you get to eat, shit, sleep, and live for free?" I looked at him with a smirk on my face.

"Damn! Destiny, what's up with this attitude? I mean, I know I haven't been able to help out, but dammit, I came to you for help when I decided to go back to school and you agreed. Now all you do is throw this shit in my face. I only have a few years left and I'm going to show you the kind of man I know I can be. Just be patient, baby. I promise, I gotchu."

I almost busted out laughing; his speech and the look on his face were priceless. This weak-ass nigga thought he had me fooled. "Listen up. I was fine helping you go back to school so you could better yourself. I carried your weight and never once did I complain, but the minute that you started sticking your cock into other bitches, that shit ended. I'm not paying no nigga's way so he has free time to go search for pussy."

I didn't wait for a response. I got up off the sofa and walked away. I felt like if I didn't, I would've kicked the shit out of his ass.

CHAPTER EIGHT

Destiny Clarke

Six Years Later
Time flew by. It seemed like it was just the other day that I met Hassan and we had our daughter, but in reality, Amaiya turned six a few days ago, and her daddy was graduating from law school. I wasn't working as hard as I used to before; I only worked three nights at the hospital. I spent all my free time doing things with my daughter.

You would've thought that our relationship would've gotten better. Instead, it only got worse. There were nights that he didn't bother to come home or even call me to say he wasn't coming home. I can't believe that I would sit in the house and call his phone back-to-back. As usual, the calls would go straight to voicemail. Many nights, I would turn to the bottle of red wine that I kept in the pantry. Other times, I would cry myself to sleep, hoping that he would change his ways and go back to being the nigga that I met.

I tried to rack my brain to get some kind of under-standing as to why he was doing me like this. I was a bad female in my eyes. I had a nice body, my pussy was tight, I sucked his dick good, and I had money.

He had barely touched me in over three months. I would try to rub on him and he would turn on his side and fall asleep. I don't care what anyone said. I know his ass was getting pussy elsewhere.

Hassan Clarke

Juggling two women and two different lives was taking
a toll on me. I had to pay Imani's ass five thousand up
front so she wouldn't call Destiny anymore. I still didn't
think her child was mine, but I couldn't risk Destiny
finding out about him. I made sure I kept her pocket full
and visited her on the regular. That made her stay quiet
for a little while.

After leaving school one day, I stopped by to check on
them. I really didn't like the hold she had on me, but if I
told her to fuck off, that would only make her mad.

"Open the door, I'm outside."

"Dang! You don't ever call before you pop up," she said,
annoyed.

"Man, shut the fuck up sometimes."

I waited for her dumb ass to open the door. She looked
at me like I was disturbing her, or some shit like that.

"What the fuck is yo' problem, yo!"

I walked past that bitch and sat on the couch beside li'l
man. Every time I went over to the house, I tried to find a
resemblance, but it just wasn't there. I wasn't a fool and
I wasn't tryna claim no child that didn't share my DNA.
Because of that, I couldn't bring myself to get close to
him in any way.

"Josiah, say hi to your daddy," she blurted out.

I wanted to say, "Bitch, stop telling him that and go
find his real daddy," but I kept it in. Instead, I looked
down at shorty and tickled him a little. He must have felt
the same way I did because he paid me no mind and went
back to playing his PS Vita.

"So why the fuck you keep popping up ova her fo'? You
a fucking married man now. Go watch that bitch pussy
and leave me the hell alone."

"Watch your mouth, B. This pussy will always be mine,
until I don't want it anymore. You need to learn to shut

your mouth sometimes, and maybe a nigga will stay around longer."

"I don't need yo' ass around. I waited six fucking years for you to leave them hoes alone and settle down and yo' ass went and married some bitch you don't even know. Yo' sister told me every damn thing. Boy I'm done wit' yo' ass for real."

"Yo, chill out. I only married this bitch for her money. How else would I be able to take care of yo' ass and move you out of the hood? Humble yo' self and you might be that bitch in a nigga life for real."

"You selling me fucking dreams. I'm not goin' sit around waiting on you to play house with that bitch and her child, while my son don't even fucking know you. You got me fucked up, son!"

"Ain't nobody playing house. I don't even touch that bitch no more. Your pussy is the only one that I want, on some real nigga shit."

Shit, I was at the point where I would say and do anything for shorty to shut the fuck up. I was almost finished with school and I needed Destiny's money to help me start my business. There was no way I was going to let Imani's big-ass mouth fuck up anything for me.

Destiny Clarke

My husband's graduation day was bittersweet. I was happy that he was finished with law school and would be able to pay some of these goddamn bills around here. His entire family came out to show their support and ate all my damn food. I tried to tolerate his family, but, boy, they were so loud and obnoxious. I really should've done my homework before I said, "I do," because being around them gave me a bad feeling. They had the nerve to say my baby looked like their side of the family. Bullshit. I don't know my side of family, but I know by my looks that she resembled me. Don't get me wrong: my husband wasn't an ugly man, but his mother and sisters looked like somebody let them out of the Bronx Zoo, not to mention their "BMW"s, short for "body made wrong." I sat there and shook my head as they talked about how proud they were of him. I had no understanding of the shit, because when we first met, he told me how he'd ask his family for their help, and they'd turn their back on him. Fast forward to his graduation, there they were, behaving like they've been there all along. I wanted to throw up all over them. This shit was fakeness in the first degree. I missed having a family, but if that was how they behaved, I'd pass on that family shit.

I walked into the kitchen to grab a few more cases of sodas for these hungry ass in-laws of mine. I was so caught up in my thoughts that I didn't notice my mother-in-law entering the kitchen.

"Tell me something, Destiny. What do my son see in yo' ass? Why he marry you?" That bitch startled me.

I was shocked that this bitch would have the balls to approach me like that. I turned around slowly and faced this gorilla-looking bitch. I took two steps closer to her face and then I spoke.

"Listen up bitch, the question should be: what did I see in your son? His ass wasn't shit until I picked him up and turned him into somebody. So bitch, the next time you want to address me, you better come correct."

"Excuse me? You think you all high and mighty, but trust me, my son is on his way. Mark my words: he will replace your high saditty ass pretty soon. Don't think he won't leave you and that child, which, by the way, I'm not sure is my grandbaby. I done told his ass to go get one of those tests so he can be sure. See, you have him all wrapped up around your finger, but I see you for the piece of trash you really are."

I was tired of this old raggedy bitch already. All kinds of crazy thoughts went through my mind. My kitchen was filled with sharp knives; I thought about getting one of them and cutting her ass up, but I quickly ignored that thought. I wasn't going to go to jail over this bitch and leave my baby out here without her mommy.

"Please, I'm asking you nicely to get the fuck out of my house before I have to throw all you leeches out of my shit. I really don't want to embarrass my husband on his big day." I showed her ass the door.

"What's going on in here? I was wondering where my two favorite ladies were, and here both of you are, spending quiet time together," he said, as he tried to kiss me.

I pushed him off me and walked out, leaving him and that bitch in the kitchen.

"Hello everyone. I'm sorry to inform y'all that the party is over. I have work in the morning and I have to straighten up this place before I call it a night," I sternly said.

Everyone turned to me with strange looks on their faces. As I stood there, looking to see if they were going to get their asses up out of my house, I felt someone grab my arm.

"What you think you're doing? This my party." He squeezed my arm tighter.

"You better let go of my fucking arm before I show my ass off in here." I pulled my arm out of his grip.

I walked over to open the door so they could get out of my damn house. One by one, they grabbed their belongings and left. Some shot me dirty looks, but I didn't give a damn about looks.

"You remember what I told you earlier. He's going to leave yo' ass real soon," his gorilla-ass mama whispered to me as she walked out the door.

I didn't even bother to reply. Instead, I slammed my door shut and walked into my dining room. I started to clean up because of the big mess. I saw Hassan shoot me a dirty look as he walked past the room. Obviously, he was upset that I put his clan out. I didn't give a fuck. This was my shit and under no circumstances was I going to let anyone come up in here and disrespect me the way his mama did. The only way that bitch would be welcome in my house was if I were dead.

That night, after cleaning up, I got my baby ready for bed. She was knocked out in no time. I took a long, hot shower and got into bed. I was beat and I had to get up for work in the morning. This twelve-hour shift at the hospital was taking a toll on me. I thought about doing fewer days in the future.

I was just about to doze off when he entered the room. I closed my eyes and pretended that I was asleep. He got into the bed and tried to hug me. I pushed his arm off—I was not in the mood to be touched. I was too tired to even dig into his ass about his mother telling him to get tested for our daughter. I think he understood because he got out the bed, grabbed his pillow, and mumbled something under his breath. I rolled over and dozed off to sleep.

CHAPTER NINE

Hassan Clarke

My big day turned into a fucking circus. I was happy that I got my degree, but I was pissed that Destiny showed her ass. See, this bitch was straight up disrespectful. She put my fucking family out of her shit. I mean, it was my shit too, but she treated them like they were trespassing. I knew my sisters were ready to whup that ass if I didn't tell them to cool. Destiny knows she ain't built like that.

I even tried to touch her ass in the bed, but she was still on her bullshit. I didn't trip; I got up, took my pillow, and pretended like I was going to sleep downstairs. See, I had a backup plan once things didn't go my way.

I dialed Tanya's number. I knew this was risky, but shit, I loved taking chances. The night was young. I was tipsy from all that drinking. Plain and simple, I wanted to fuck.

"Hello," her sultry voice echoed through the phone.

"What you doing? Been thinking 'bout you all day," I lied.

"Really, I couldn't get you out my mind since you left that day. I thought you forgot about me when I didn't hear from you."

"Nah, shorty, how could I forget 'bout a beautiful lady like yo'self? I just been ripping and running a little."

"Oh, you're too sweet. I want to see you again."

"Shit, that's what I called you for. I'm over here by my sister's house and was wondering if you wanted to come through for a minute?"

"Of course. I want to see you."

I gave her the address before hanging up.

Tanya was the paralegal that I met on campus the other day. Fine little white chick with a Southern accent. I've never had a woman outside of my race before, so I decided to try my hand. Shit, it worked; she invited me to her apartment over on Gramatan Avenue and before I knew it, she had all nine inches of my dick in her mouth. Yo, shorty was a beast with that mouth, and she swallowed every drop of my cum. Needless to say, I burned that young pussy up. I had her screaming "Daddy," the entire time.

In no time, Tanya was pulling up in the driveway. I motioned for her to pull to the side. That way, her car wasn't visible from upstairs. I walked into the living room with her in hot pursuit.

"We got to hold it down, 'cause my sister isn't feeling well and I don't want to wake her up."

"Oh, okay. I understand. Is she all right?" she said, sounding concerned.

"Yeah, I think she has a stomach virus and she's been up all day, so we have to be extra quiet. You feel me?"

"Sure."

Those words were the last ones we spoke. We got straight down to business. I ate her pussy up and she devoured my dick. I fucked her from the back and she rode me on the couch. There was something about that young pussy that drove me to a level I'd never experienced before. I had to try my damnedest not to let out any sound, and I had to use my hand to cover her moans. It didn't take me long to bust. This time, I made sure I pulled out and bust into my hands. There was no way I was taking any more chances. I went into the downstairs bathroom and handed her a wet washcloth; she wiped herself, got dressed, and left.

I went into the bathroom and washed myself off, then poured myself a glass of Hennessy and went into the living room. I drank the liquor and watched a little TV until I dozed off, thinking about that piece of pussy that I just burned up.

CHAPTER TEN

Destiny Clarke

I was a damn fool for thinking Hassan graduating would change our situation. He tried to get a job with a reputable law firm, but that didn't work out. I saw the frustration on his face after each interview, which resulted in him being sullen and angry. I had to figure out something real fast. Even though his ass was doing me wrong, I loved him and wanted to see him prosper.

"Hey, babe, you ever thought about starting your own company?"

"No, I've never thought about it. Besides, I don't have that kind of money to start no firm," he said in a distressed tone.

"I don't see why not. You are good at what you do. Furthermore, you will be your own boss and you can find a few other lawyers to join you."

"Goddamn, Destiny, I just told yo' ass that I ain't got no damn money to start no firm," he yelled.

I looked at this nigga like what the fuck? Here I was trying to help this fool, but he was too ignorant to see that. The thing I hated the most was an educated dummy and I had to admit my husband was an educated nigga, who was dumb as fuck.

"Calm yo' ass down! What I was trying to say is that I will help you with the money to start your own company.

Shit, I'll even work as the secretary until you can afford to hire one."

"Damn, babe, why didn't you say that then, instead of beating around the damn bush?" he smiled.

"Mommy, Mommy, come look at SpongeBob on my TV," my princess yelled before I had a chance to answer this fool.

Amaiya grabbed my hand and tried to pull me upstairs with her. Her innocence was so amazing. Sometimes I wondered where I would be if I didn't have this little girl.

"Sit down, Mommy."

"Okay, baby girl."

I sat down and hugged my baby girl tight. Deep down I was hurting; I had no idea why this nigga talked so crazy to the only person that was really in his corner. Even through the stress and aggravation, I still loved him and really wanted to hold my family together. I looked down at my princess who by now had fallen asleep. If nothing else, I wanted to give her the world and that included keeping her daddy around.

After a few minutes, I laid her down on the bed, pulled the blanket over her, and kissed her goodnight. I turned the television off and left her.

Hassan was in my room, sprawled across the bed. I started to turn around, but then he hollered my name.

"Destiny, come over here."

"What is it? I got to clean up the kitchen," I lied.

"Fuck that, it can wait. Come here, babe."

I walked over and sat at the edge of the bed.

Hassan got up, walked over to me, and knelt down before me. The only things that came out of his mouth were lies, so I had no idea what he wanted.

"Babe, I know I haven't been much of a man to you lately and I need to get back on my shit. Destiny, I love you so much. It's just the stress of not being able to provide for you and Amaiya. I'm a man and that's what I should do—provide."

"You know what, Hassan? It has never been about the money with me. Shit, I make my own money. The shit that bothers me is the way you've changed. We don't spend any time together. You're barely home and on the days that you are, you barely spend any time with me and your daughter. You're always angry like I did some grimy shit to you."

"Babe, I know and I apologize. Man, babe, you and baby girl is the best thing that ever happened to me. I longed for a family of my own all my life and here I have it. I need to tighten up some. I promise, babe. From this day on, I won't disrespect you anymore. I swear, you're my queen and I will start treating you like you deserve."

I didn't say anything. Instead, I sat there looking at him. I've heard these lies from him before. I wasn't going to say he couldn't change because any man can change if they really want to. Key word—want.

Before I could finish my thoughts, he spread my legs, pulled my underwear off, and dug his head in between my legs. I shivered with pleasure as soon as his tongue connected with my clit.

Oh how I miss this, I thought as he gripped my clit aggressively with his lips and tongue.

"*Aargh*," I screamed out in ecstasy.

He tightened his lock as he sucked my pussy with passion. I screamed louder, but was careful not to wake up my baby.

"Come here. Come give me this dick," I begged.

"Nah, no dick. You've been a naughty girl. You don't deserve this," he teased.

I was getting irritated because my pussy was on fire and I needed a cock to cool it down.

He sucked harder as I climaxed and my body shivered uncontrollably.

"Please, daddy, come fuck me. Please."

"I tell you what; tell daddy that you going to give him the money for the firm and I might give you some of this good dick."

"Man, yes. Whatever you want, you can get," I screamed out.

"Anything?" He sucked harder.

"How 'bout a threesome?"

"What the fuck you mean by a threesome? I'm not fucking no other nigga." I looked at him, shocked as hell.

"Nah, babe, I wasn't talking 'bout you fucking no other nigga. I was talking 'bout me, you and another female."

"What the fuck kind of request is that? You think I would sit around and watch you fuck another bitch in front of me? Boy, you done lost your fucking mind!" I pushed him away from me.

"Damn, babe, you acting like I just asked you the worst shit in the world. I know quite a few niggas who had another bitch with their girl in bed. It's no big deal."

I stood up and stepped closer to his face.

"'No big deal.' You want to bring another bitch into our bed and here you are telling me that it's no big deal. I love cock, not pussy. I wasn't raised like that. Listen up, nigga: if you feel the need for some new pussy, you need to get a fucking divorce and go get you a bitch that doesn't mind sucking on another bitch's pussy. I am not the fucking one."

I grabbed my pillow and my blanket and walked out of the room. I couldn't believe this fucking nigga just asked me that shit. I don't know what the fuck this nigga was on if he thought that I would be down with some shit like that. I locked the door to the guestroom and crawled into the bed. The tears started to flow. When it wasn't one thing, it was another. *God help me*, I thought as I dozed off.

***

The way I loved that man was crazy. I cried for days after he asked about a damn threesome. It never seemed to bother him. Instead, he continued to press the issue. I saw he wasn't letting up any, so I finally decided to try it out. I felt like I was out of my mind to even give in to such a demand, but I didn't want to lose him and since it seemed like everybody done tried that shit, I decided to do it.

"Listen, I'll have the threesome with you and the other person," I said.

His face lit up instantly. It was that moment that I saw him for the dog that he really was. He didn't give a fuck about me or my feelings. I shook my head in disbelief as he sat across from me at the dinner table.

"Babe, listen, I know that it took e'erything in you to do this for me. I love you girl, and I want you to know I ain't leaving you for no bitch. You my woman, you hear me?"

I continued chewing on the piece of steak without saying a single word. All I could think about was another woman fucking my husband in front of me. I instantly felt sick. I got up and rushed to the bathroom on the first floor. I threw up the entire meal that I had consumed minutes earlier.

God, what have I gotten myself into, I thought.

"You all right in there sweetheart?" his voice interrupted my thoughts.

"Yes, think I had too much to eat. I'll be out shortly."

I brushed my teeth, washed my face with cold water, dried my tears with a towel, and walked out of the bathroom.

After a few days of not talking to Hassan, he finally asked me out to dinner. I was still upset with him, but

I did not like when we were not talking. I agreed to do dinner with him because it had been a while since we had gone out anywhere. I put on a pair of Levi's Jeans, a sleeveless top I got from Macy's, and a pair of Michael Kors sandals. He didn't say where we were going, so I dressed casual. I looked myself over in the mirror and instantly noticed all the bags underneath my eyes. It seemed as if I'd aged ten years. I quickly turned away from the truth that was staring me dead in the face. I snatched up my clutch, turned the lights off, and walked out of the room.

"Sweetheart, why do you look like that? Everything all right?" he asked, startling me.

"Yes, I'm fine," I smiled at him.

I was caught up in my feelings because deep down, I knew he was full of shit, but what was crazy was the fact that that my dumb ass was still in love with him. I'd thought about leaving him so many times, but something held me back. I needed to wake the fuck up, or this man was going to drag me down with him. We sat in the dimly lit area in the back section of the restaurant. It wasn't too fancy, but then again, Hassan's behind was cheap as hell. We ate and I drank two glasses of Bahama Mama's, which were enough for me because I started to feel lightheaded. He paid the waitress and we left at around 9:30 p.m.

I was tired and was ready to lie down and catch an episode of *Blue Bloods* on TV. The ride home was quiet. I would've given anything to know what was going on in his mind. He must have read my thoughts because seconds later he spoke up. "Destiny. . . Umm. . . Baby. . . What about that threesome tonight? I've been patiently waiting." He glanced at me.

"So, this is what it was all about? That's why you asked me out to dinner. Because you want me to eat another bitch's pussy and watch you fuck her? Nigga, fuck you! I could have bought my own dinner!" I screamed.

I was so fucking angry, I started to tremble.

"Baby, calm down. I don't like when you get this mad. You start sounding like one of these hood rat bitches around here. That shit don't fit you."

I was going to dig into his ass, but I was quickly reminded of my mama's words: "If you know better, than you'll do better." I took a deep breath and turned my head toward the street. The rest of the ride was quiet and minutes later we pulled up at home. I couldn't wait to get out of the car, but before I could do so, he grabbed my arm.

"Sit down, babe." He took his hand and turned my face toward him.

"Destiny, man what's happening between us? You seem so angry at me. What, you 'ont love a nigga no more? 'Cause I've been in love with you from the day I laid eyes on you. Ain't nothing changed on my end."

"Really? Because you know I don't feel any of that. You come and go as you please. You act like you not married. Shit, you barely spent any time with your child. So how do you love me?"

"I know I've been slipping, but it don't have nothing to do with me not loving you. I'm just stressed out. How do you think I feel, knowing that my woman is the bread-winner? I'm supposed to be taking care of my woman and showering her with gifts, not the other way around. I love you, woman, with everything in me. Listen, give me a chance to show you how much you mean to me," he said.

Tears rolled down his face. I'd never seen him cry before and it definitely melted my heart. He looked me in the eyes as he professed his love to me, crying his heart out. I hugged him tight as he continued talking. In the midst of all that, his phone started ringing. I watched as he scooted back and looked at the caller ID.

Hmm...I wonder who the hell was blowing him up like that.

"Who was that?"

"Oh, that was the chick that I was telling you about. She 'bout to pull up."

"Really? You made plans without telling me. How you know I was down for a shift tonight?"

"Babe, listen, please do this for me. One time. I promise I'll never ask you to do it again. It's always been a fantasy of mine and I want to share that moment with my wife." I sat there in silence. I felt like this was all bullshit he was feeding me to get his way, but on the other hand, I wanted to be the woman that would do anything to make her husband happy.

"All right, just this one time. Don't you ask me to do this shit no more." I snatched my arm away and got out of the car. *The nerve of this man,* I thought as I opened the door.

I didn't know how it was going to turn out, so I went upstairs to take a shower. All kinds of crazy thoughts ran through my mind as the water pounded on my body. The thought of being with another woman turned my stomach. I didn't knock anyone's choices, but I grew up believing a man was for a woman and a woman for a man. I got out of the shower, dried off, and put on my Victoria's Secret Dream Angels body lotion and, afterward, my nightgown.

Then I heard voices downstairs. This nigga was dead-ass serious. I was hoping it was a bluff. I pranced downstairs and stumbled into the living room, where the voices were coming from.

I stood in a trance, lost for words, as I noticed a white bitch on her knees with my husband's cock in her mouth.

"What are you doing?" I leaped toward her.

"This is Tanya, the chick that I was telling you about. She was just getting me ready."

"Getting you ready? That's what you call getting your cock sucked in my living room."

"I'm lost. I thought you said she was down with it." This little slut managed to pick up her mouth off his cock long enough to speak up.

I stepped closer to her, fully intending to smack the life out of her, but Hassan jumped in between us.

"Tell me, you little cracker bitch, how long have you been fucking my husband?"

"Husband?"

She turned to Hassan with a confused look plastered across her face.

"Uh. . . Uh. . . Calm down. You didn't give me a chance to tell you," he stuttered.

"So I ask you again, how long have you and my husband been screwing around?"

"Come on, Destiny. Quit harassing this young girl like that."

I took a step closer to this fuck-nigga's face.

"Shut the fuck up. This is a grown-ass ho; a few minutes ago, she was on her knees sucking your cock. That alone lets me know she's a grown-ass ho. So before you try to check behind a ho, get your shit right." I poked him in the face with my finger.

"Yo chill out, putting yo' hands on me like that. You agreed to this, now you in here actin' a fucking fool."

"Listen, lady, I had no idea he was married. I met him at school and we dating. I've been over here before and I had no idea he had a woman." She smirked at him.

"Bitch, shut your damn mouth." He grabbed her neck.

"Let her go! Ain't no need for your ass to get mad. This is what you wanted to do, remember?"

He let go of her neck. I watched as she gasped for air.

"Now that the show is over, why don't you take your whore and get out my house!"

"What do you mean get out your house? This is my shit too."

"You cheatin' ass bastard, you heard me. Get your little whore and get the fuck out of my shit before I call the fucking police. You know once they come, one of us got to go and this is my shit, so I ain't going nowhere." I looked at him, and he knew I was dead-ass serious; there wasn't a hint of a smile on my face.

The bitch got the picture, because she grabbed her things and walked away.

"Babe, it ain't like that. That bitch lying on me, I swear to you."

"Hassan, you know, you can't even keep a straight face when you lying. I'm done with you. Please get your shit and get out my house. I mean it. Trust me, I can do bad by my damn self." I stormed off.

I heard the front door open and a car pull off. I figured I was not the only mad bitch. *Oh well*, I thought as I walked up the stairs, fuming. This bastard had this little bitch up in my house. How low could this nigga stoop, after all that I'd done for him? The tears began to flow, my chest tightened up, and my mouth gathered water. I rushed to the toilet and threw up everything I ate earlier. I brushed my teeth and washed my face. This didn't make any kind of sense and the tears continued to flow. I lay across the bed with my face buried in my pillow. "God, why does this man continue to treat me like this?" I asked out loud.

***

Last night was hell. I tossed and turned all night. I also noticed Hassan's car was gone. I got up, took a shower, and made a cup of tea and toast. My head was pounding from all the crying that I did last night. I grabbed the bottle of Aleve and took two pills to help ease the headache. It was Sunday and my baby girl was still at my mom's house. I decided to get dressed and go see Mama.

In no time, I was pulling up in front of her house. I parked, grabbed my purse, and walked up to the driveway. "Ooh, it's chilly," I mumbled. My ass ran out of the house without grabbing my jacket.

I knocked on the door, shivering.

"Who is it, banging on my damn door like that?" she yelled.

"It's me, Mama."

She opened the door and stood in the doorway, looking at me like I was trespassing.

"It's cold out here," I said, as I pushed past her.

"You damn right! Only a fool walk around here without a coat like it's summer time." She locked the door.

"Where's my baby?"

"She asleep. I gave her a nice bath and fed her some oatmeal. Before I knew it, she was out cold."

I walked into the living room and dropped down on the couch.

"Why you here? I thought you said you were going to get here later on."

"I know, but I needed to get out the house."

"Child, you look like you been to hell and back. Are you all right?"

At first, I didn't respond. I sat there staring out into space. Mama and I were close, but I didn't let her know about my personal business. After all, what could she really say? She had stayed with that bastard, washing, cooking, and being the good army wife.

"Child, say something. You scaring the hell out of me."

I looked at her and instantly the tears poured out. She walked over to me and sat down.

"Baby, talk to me. Did somebody hurt you? Talk to me." She hugged me.

I didn't respond. Instead, I started bawling louder.

"Destiny, if you don't tell me, I can't help you. Is it Hassan? Did he hurt you?"

"Mom it's okay," I mumbled.

"Like hell it is. Not when you sit on my damn couch bawling your eyes out. That bastard better not do anything to my child, 'cause he'll have to deal with me."

Mama was nothing but a good 4'9", but she had a big voice that would make you tremble when she yelled. I picked my head up and wiped my nose. As I glanced at Mama, I realized that she wasn't going to ease up. Reluctantly, I told her a little of what was going on. I didn't tell her everything because I was a bit embarrassed about some of the things that were going on. When I was finished, Mama got up and stood in front of me.

"Let me tell you something: don't repeat the mistakes I made. You are too strong of a woman to let this boy treat you like you are a doormat. You picked him up and turned him into somebody and now his ungrateful behind want to show his ass. Child, I can't tell you how to live your life, but you need to do what's best for you and Amaiya."

"That's the point Mama. That's her daddy. I don't want to take her away from him." The tears began flowing again.

She sat down beside me, took my hand and placed it in hers. "Child, cut out the foolishness. You don't have to be with him for him to be in his child's life. Don't you be like me and stay with a man because of convenience."

"So you're saying you stayed with a man because of convenience?" I looked at her.

"Sure I did. The love died a long time ago after he started sleeping with all those other woman in different states. Those army men are pure sluts. I stayed with him because he made good money and the benefits were nice. It was only after I found out what he did to you that I decided to leave him. I couldn't stand to be in the same room with that bastard after all that happened."

I squeezed her hand. Mama hadn't thought twice when all that shit went down. She divorced him and we moved away.

"Anyway, enough about me. I've lived my life. Now it's you that need to decide what you going to do."

I looked at her. I wished I could give her the answer. Truth is, deep down, I loved him and I always imagined us together forever, but his disrespectful ass done crossed the line.

"Mommy, Mommy, Mommy," Amaiya hollered as she ran into the room, jumping on me.

"Hey baby."

"Mommy, what's wrong? Why Mommy cry?"

I quickly wiped my tears and smiled at her. "Baby, there's something in my eyes."

"Let me blow, then." She tried to pry my eye open.

"It's already out," I lied.

"Maiya, let's get some juice," Mama said.

"Now wipe your tears and get yourself together. All them damn tears won't change a thing if you're still in the same situation," she scolded me before walking out with Amaiya.

I leaned my head back and closed my eyes. As harsh as her words seemed, she was right.

Lord, I need you right now, I thought. I wiped my tears and continued to lie there. I was tired and mentally drained. *I can't do this anymore*, I thought before I dozed off.

Hassan Clarke

The bitch that I married was one step away from becoming psychotic. How the fuck she goin' agree to have a threesome, then wait 'til I bring the bitch over to get all emotional and shit? I was mad as fuck when she interrupted me. See, these bitches didn't know when to shut the fuck up. Destiny's ass was at the top of the line of being disrespectful. She had the nerve to put me out. At first I wasn't going anywhere, then I was like what the fuck, she did me a favor. As soon as I pulled out of the driveway, I called Imani. "What the fuck you want this time of night?" she asked me with attitude.

"Yo, watch your mouth. I'm on the way over there."

"Whatever." She hung up the phone.

Oh hell no, I might end up beating her ass. It's bad enough I had to deal with one disrespectful bitch, but another one was out of the question. I banged on the door with frustration.

"Who is it?" she hollered.

"Open the fucking door, yo."

She popped open the door with an attitude plastered across her face. I pushed past her and walked into the living room.

"Where's my son at?"

"He's asleep, what you think? I want to know what breeze blew you over here this time of night. Better yet, do your wife know where the fuck you at?"

"Come on with all this questioning. It don't matter if she know or not. I'm a grown-ass man, I'll go where the hell I want to go."

"Boy whatever! Don't come up in here acting like you run shit. This is my muthafucking house. So act like you know it."

I was tired of hearing this bitch yap her cock suckers. I walked off on that ass, went into the bedroom, grabbed a pillow, went to the couch, and lay down. She must have gotten the picture, because she walked off cussing under her breath, and then slammed her bedroom door.

I kicked my sneakers off and lay back down. My phone started buzzing and I looked at the screen. It was Tanya's ass. "Hell no," I blurted out. I pressed the ignore button and cut my phone off. Enough was enough.

Imani Gibson

This nigga thought it was cool to pop up at my crib like he fucking owns me. Honestly, I was sick and tired of all the bullshit he was dishing out. Yes, I took the money he gave me at first, but deep down, that shit didn't mean anything at all. He couldn't continue to give me money to keep my mouth shut and hide my son from his bitch; he must not know me. There was no way me and my child were going to roll over and stay quiet. If he knew what I knew, he'd hurry up and get rid of that ho before shit hit the fan. Lord knows I was tired of my baby asking for his daddy and me having to lie to him, telling him his daddy was away working. Having to lie to my little man hurt my heart. Trust me, it was about to get real.

My phone started ringing; it was Hassan's sister.

"Hey bitch."

"Hey yourself. You heard what happened?" I sat on the edge of the bed, because I knew she had some drama to share.

"Nah, what you talking about that?"

"That bitch put my brother out of the house. I overheard him and Mama talking earlier."

"I guess there's trouble in paradise after all."

"Girl, I can't stand that ho. I can't wait till the day when my brother leaves her alone."

"You know your brother ain't going nowhere 'cause that bitch got money."

"That shit don't mean nothing. He got his degree now, so it's easier now for him to leave that trifling-ass heffer alone."

I remained quiet. I was digesting everything I was hearing. It all made sense now. "Anyway, how's my nephew? I bought him some clothes. Target had a sale so I grabbed him a few outfits. I'ma come through tomorrow."

"Good. He's asleep. But I'll be here tomorrow. All you and your mama do is spoil him, always buying him things."

"Somebody has to do it. As far as me and my mom is concerned, he's the only sure one. That bitch's daughter is suspect. Mama keep telling him to get a damn blood test, but his hardheaded ass still ain't listen. One of these damn days, I'm going to get the little girl and buy one of those DNA tests at CVS and swab her behind. My brother's not going to like it when I expose the truth, but oh well. He'll thank me in the long run."

Yeah, well, he'll be aiight," I said.

"Anyway bitch, I gotta run. I'll see you tomorrow."

"Aiight boo. See you then."

I didn't mean to be short with my bitch, but my mind was occupied with the information she'd just dished out.

The next day, his sister came through as promised. She brought my son the stuff she bought for him. He loved whenever his auntie visited. In fact, no matter how badly has Hassan treated me, his family has always treated me well, especially his mom and sister. His mother always told me how much her son loves me and she wished I were his wife. I think she has no idea that her son is a two-timing ass nigga that didn't know what he wanted.

"Was that my brother pulling out, when I was pulling in?"

"Damn bitch, you 'ont miss a beat. Yeah, that was him."

"And that's why your ass acting all happy and shit. I hope you ain't fucking him."

"Damn bitch, if I was, it's my pussy and that's my baby daddy, remember?" I said, annoyed.

"Damn, pump your brakes, boo. I know it's your pussy. All I'm saying is, as long as you keep opening your legs to him, he going to continue using you and go home to his wife. Is this how you want to live your life?"

"You know what, Charmaine? Not everybody has a man like yours. Some of us bitches are not that lucky. Me and Hassan have been messing around for four years. Then this bitch came along. So why does it seem like he's her man and I'm in the wrong? No, Hassan has always been my man and my son's father. I put up with his shit, so I deserve to have him."

"But listen to me. I love you like a sister and I would do anything for you, but like you said, y'all been messing around. He knows he can fuck any and everything that has a pussy, and you'll still be around waiting. You deserve better. I love my brother too, but he's a player."

"I hear you."

"Well, I gotta run. I'll call you." She kissed Josiah and left.

I slammed the door and took a deep breath. I loved her so damn much, but she always felt the need to preach to me. Fuck, I didn't want to hear that shit and I refused to sit back and let this bitch play wifey.

The next couple of days were crazy. I got up every morning, cooked Hassan and my son a big breakfast, then at night I would suck his dick like my life depended on it, and I would ride that dick with everything in me. Not once did I mention his bitch or even fuss at him. My son was also happy to have his daddy here with him; if nothing else, I was glad that my son was happy. After about two weeks of us playing house, I noticed Hassan seemed distant. I knew he said he was trying to find a job at different law firms, so I figured that was stressing him out. But his attitude got worse each day that went by. Things took a turn for the worse when I tried to rub on him one night.

"Nah B, not tonight. I'm beat."

"Really?" I blurted out.

I rolled to one side of the bed and stayed there. I didn't know what brought on his attitude, but I knew it had something to do with that bitch.

The next morning, I got up and cooked breakfast as usual, then I sat down at the table with my baby. I heard Hassan moving around. I looked up as he walked in the dining room.

"Hey babe," I greeted him.

"Listen, we need to talk," he said sternly.

"Yeah, wassup?" I asked.

"I came here 'cause Destiny and I had a fight and she put me out. Truth is, I need her to help me start this firm. I can't just walk away from all that."

"So what the fuck are you saying? Just fucking spit it out, yo," I yelled.

"See, that's what I'm talking about. You can't shut up long enough. This is it right here. I know you love a nigga and trust I love yo' ass too, but I need you to be a little more patient. I promise that I'll leave her ass as soon as I get this business on the ground."

"How many times you going to preach these lies? I've been waiting on you for all these fucking years and you went off to marry some random bitch. Boy, I'm so over you and your bullshit," I yelled.

"Man I know I done dragged you through the mud, but don't no other bitch have my heart. I fucking love you

Mani. All I'm asking is for you to chill out a little longer. We on our way to the top, baby. The top, you hear me? Me, you, and my son."

He got up, walked over to me, and kissed me passionately.

"Stop. Josiah's right there," I mumbled.

"Li'l man, sit and eat. I need to talk wit' yo' mama real quick."

He grabbed my hand and pulled me into the room. Like a savage animal, he ripped my T-shirt and boy shorts off. He picked me up in the air and dug into my pussy. He sucked my clit so damn good, it sent me into a euphoric state.

"*Woiee*," I screamed out in ecstasy. The harder he sucked on my clit, the louder I screamed.

I had no idea what had gotten into him, but whatever his motivation was, I loved it. After I climaxed and he licked up every drop of juice, he put me on the bed and slowly fucked me. I swear, I fell in love with him all over again. He fucked my mind and my soul.

"Mama, you okay?" I heard Josiah holler.

"Yes baby. Go sit down and watch cartoons."

Hassan didn't ease up any; he continued to serenade my body. Moments later, we both came together. It was beautiful and he held me tightly afterwards.

"Listen B, I got to go back to the house for a little while longer, so I can get things together."

"Aiight, but don't take too long. I want you here with us, not over there with that bitch. She don't know how to love you like I do," I assured him.

"I know baby, daddy got you."

He got up, put on his boxers and walked out the room. I lay on the bed thinking, *I hope he was for real this time, because a bitch is tired of playing these people's side bitch games.*

CHAPTER ELEVEN

Destiny Clarke

Days went by without hearing a word from Hassan. I understood that I put his ass out, but his child was still here. I refused to call him; I hadn't done anything wrong and there was no way I was going to pretend that I had.

Two weeks passed and still no word and I couldn't take it anymore because my child kept asking for her daddy. I tried his number and it kept going to voicemail. Reluctantly, I dialed his mama's number, and after a few rings, she picked up.

"Hello," she yelled into the phone.

The nerve of this woman, I thought.

"This Destiny. I'm looking for your son. I was wondering if you've seen him?"

"I know who you is and no. You're married to him, so you should know where he's at," she spat.

"Listen lady, I ain't call you for all this."

"No, you listen to me you little tramp. You called my phone looking for my son. I see you not the main one, 'cause if you was, you'd know where your husband is. I don't know, he might be wrapped up with his latest fling," she chuckled.

"You know what, fuck you, you ignorant-ass heffer." I clicked the phone off.

I took a few deep breaths. I was fuming. This bitch was nothing short of a fucking parasite. I didn't even like fighting, but I swear, I could wrap my hands around that big bitch's neck. I got up and went to the kitchen, poured me a glass of pink Moscato, gulped it down and followed up with another glass.

I was hurting inside and didn't want to be around anyone so I took a few days off work. Amaiya was at school and I decided to do some cleaning up to get my mind off things. I was in the kitchen cleaning when I heard the front door open. I hurriedly walked toward the door and saw it was my so-called husband. I tried to turn away as soon as I saw him.

"Destiny, we need to talk," he yelled.

"Talk. . . talk about what? I hope you're here to get your clothes."

"Get my clothes? Are you saying you're done? 'cause I ain't going nowhere."

"Hassan, you left for three weeks, and not once did you call or stop by to check on your child. But, here you are, talking about you ain't going nowhere. In my book, you already left."

"Nah babe, you was pissed the fuck off and I didn't want to upset you anymore. All I did was leave until you calmed down a little bit. Woman I love you, why would I want to leave you and my daughter?"

"Really? Oh and yeah, your mama said you was with one of your bitches. You know what, it might be that bitch you been fucking."

"Come on Destiny, you know damn well my mama don't like you and will say anything to mess us up. I wasn't with no other woman. I was over my boy's crib over in Co-op City."

"Yeah right! I don't even know you. You're so different than the man I married. You violated me in the worst way by bringing that bitch up in my house. Not in a million years would I think that you would do me like that." I tried my best not to cry, but my heart was broken and the tears flowed out.

"Baby, come here, I apologize wit' e'erything in me. I know I fucked up, but I can't leave you alone. Woman, you're my everything." He stepped closer to me and tried to touch me.

"Don't touch me!" I said. I ran up the stairs and slammed the door. I crawled underneath my covers. I was beyond hurt. This man shattered my soul into tiny molecules. I lay there thinking of how to get out of this fucked up relationship.

I was a strong woman; at least I thought so, before I started messing with Hassan. He kept apologizing and even offered to get counseling. At first, I was holding out, but I'm a woman that believes that anyone can change their ways. I decided to forgive my husband and to give our marriage another try. I loved him and didn't want to lose him. I also didn't want Amaiya to live without her daddy.

Mama said I was a damn fool for taking him back, but I wasn't trying to hear that shit. She had already lived her life and I'll be damned if I was going to be old and lonely.

Things changed tremendously over the next few months. Whatever that therapist was saying to Hassan was definitely working. He was helping out around the house and spending quality time with his daughter. Breakfast would be ready when I got home from work. To top it off, he would set my bath water and wash me from head to toe. I loved the new Hassan. He was a changed man and I was happy.

We also took a vacation to Negril, Jamaica and enjoyed ourselves. The time that we spent together definitely strengthened our bond. The two weeks came and went, and our vacation was over. It was time to get back to our regular lives. I only hoped the wave would last.

Soon as we got back to the U.S., Hassan asked me if I was willing to help him with his law firm. I was a little reluctant at first because I still didn't completely trust him. That was a lot of money to give someone, whether it was my husband or not. I told him to give me a few days to think about it. He surprised me when he didn't get upset. Instead, he said "okay" and kissed me on the forehead.

Instead of giving Hassan the money, I decided to invest in the business. That way, if something happened, I would be able to recoup my money. I wrote him a check for $40,000, which was money that I had saved up for my retirement. He found an office building. It wasn't a big one, but it was good for someone starting out. He also found an attorney who was looking for a partner and he brought his clientele. Hassan might not have had the experience, but he learned fast and in no time the clients were pouring in. Word spread that this young, talented attorney could talk his way out of any situation. They hired a paralegal and I volunteered to be the secretary until they were able to hire one. It was hard on me because I worked at the firm in the daytime and the hospital at night. Furthermore, I was spending less time with Amaiya. At times, Mama had to step in and help me out by picking her up from school. Mama didn't understand the reasoning behind me helping Hassan, but I was a rider for my husband.

I popped in one day while he was in court; I wanted to see what everyone was talking about. I watched as my husband performed—he was a natural and had a gift of gab. I watched as the jurors hung on to every word he spit out.

The workload was getting heavier and we decided it was time for the firm to get a secretary. I put an ad in the newspaper and also promoted it on Facebook. I got to the office earlier than usual so I could straighten up a little because he had an appointment for the secretary position.

"Good morning. I'm here for the interview. My name is Imani Gibson," this dark-skinned woman in an extra tight skirt said.

"Good morning, I'm Mrs. Clarke. Mr. Clarke is going to conduct the interview. He's on the telephone, but I'll let him know you're here. Please have a seat."

If I wasn't mistaken, I could've sworn I saw a smirk on her face while I was talking. A bad feeling came over me and I looked at her from head to toe. She was dressed more for the club, instead of an interview for an office job.

I buzzed Hassan to let him know his ten a.m. appointment was here. Within seconds, he emerged from his office. I watched as he walked in; he seemed a little nervous. He greeted the young lady and they walked off into his office.

I sat at my desk. Something didn't feel right about that girl, but I shook it off. Our life was going great and I wouldn't dare let my insecurities mess it up.

"Honey, Ms. Gibson got the job. She's very well-qualified and is a perfect match for the company."

"Welcome to the team." I shook her hand and she gripped my hand tightly. I quickly pulled my hand away from her.

CHAPTER TWELVE

Imani Gibson

If you want something in life, you have to go after it. I'd been a go-getter from a young age. Mama was a dope fiend, so most days the fridge was empty. I learned to survive by any means necessary back then. I was tired of struggling though, and Hassan was living the high and mighty life with his ho, while my son and I were struggling off the little chump change he was throwing at us.

This nigga had no idea I knew where he lived. That's a man for you, dumb as hell. One day, after he left the house, I jumped in my car and followed him. I pulled up by the curb and watched as he opened the door to his brick house. A far cry from the little two-bedroom apartment he had his son and I staying in. I sat outside for a minute and then I pulled off. My mind was racing. This bitch had no idea who she was fucking with. There was no way I was going to sit back and let her enjoy what rightfully belonged to me.

I headed to his mother's house; his sister also lived there. Anytime I needed to know what was going on with Hassan, she was always my go-to person. I pulled up, parked, and got out of the car. I rang the doorbell and Ms. Clarke answered the door.

"Hey sugar." She gave me a hug.

I followed her into the living room and hung my coat up.

"Where's my grandson?"

"He's at school. That boy is a handful, I need a break."

"Yeah, I understand. His daddy was the same way."

"I can imagine. He still stubborn."

"Girl, just imagine how it's goin' be when Josiah grow up. I'm telling you, you goin' have to put your feet down early."

"Yeah, I be popping his ass, so he know not to fool with me."

"Is Charmaine here? I ain't see her car out front."

"She up in her room. Her tail might be on that darn Facebook. Y'all young people ain't got nun' else to do these days."

I went up the stairs and banged on her door.

"Who is it?"

"It's Mani, bitch. I'm coming in." I opened the door and walked in.

"How long you been here?"

"Just got here few minutes ago."

"Okay, what's good though?"

"Nothing, I knew it was your off day, so I decided to stop by."

"Yeah, Macy's be working me like a fucking slave. I'm ready to say fuck them. I was tempted to go get a job at my brother's firm, but I decided not to. That bitch be tripping and I swear I be ready to lay hands on her."

"Shit, if I was you, I would get the job. Fuck that bitch, that's your motherfucking brother."

"Yeah, but that's Hassan's money pit and I don't want to be the reason he loses everything before he get what he wants. Trust me, as soon as my brother gets what he want, that ho will be history. I can't fucking wait."

"That's if he leave. Hassan lies so damn much that I don't know what to believe anymore."

"I feel you, but I know my brother and I know he's only using that bitch to get what he want. My brother a player, but he ain't no fool."

We went on to talk about some other things that was going on around the neighborhood. I then decided to bounce. Charmaine was an information machine. She always had the juice on her brother. Sometimes I couldn't help but wonder if she purposely spilled the juice so I could leave him alone. Whatever her motives were, I loved hearing the latest gossip.

I got in my car and turned on the radio. I could barely hear the music through the static that blasted through my speakers. It was definitely time for an upgrade. I was tired of driving this 2006 Ford Taurus. I was ready to upgrade to something bigger and better. I listened to the words of the song as I plotted on my next move. I chuckled to myself at the thought that just popped into my head. I was a project chick, but I was far from a stupid chick. I was a freaking genius, but then again, seeing was believing.

Hassan Clarke

My heart almost stopped when my wife buzzed and said:"Imani Gibson is here for an interview.""Oh hell no, this has to be a joke," I whispered to myself. But, if I thought it was a joke then, the joke was definitely on me. I almost snapped when I saw this bitch sitting in the waiting room. I caught myself and played it off smoothly.

"Hello Ms. Gibson, I'm Hassan Clarke. Please follow me to my office."

I ushered her into my office and closed the door.

"What the fuck you think you're doing, coming up in here like this?" I grabbed her arm.

"Chill out. Y'all hiring for a receptionist and I need a job. Right?" she smirked at me.

I swear it took everything in me not to snap.

"Listen, that's my wife out there. This is dangerous, you coming in here like that."

"I won't tell if you won't. But, seriously, I need a job. That little chump change you giving me is not cutting it."

I didn't want to risk Destiny hearing us, so I tried to calm down.

"Okay, you win, but you have to keep yo' mouth shut. I can't risk you fucking up shit for me. You hear me?" I gritted my teeth at her.

I was nervous and sweating. This was too close for comfort. I walked to my desk and started the so-called interview process. I stared at Imani and saw that she was enjoying this charade a little too much. After about twenty minutes, I got up and opened the office door. She walked out, smiling from ear-to-ear.

I informed Destiny that she was now the new receptionist for the company. I watched as both women shook hands. What would have excited me at one time, made me very nervous. Imani was a ticking time bomb that I was afraid might go off at any minute. I had to hurry up and get her out of the office. I took a deep breath as she exited the building.

"You all right? You look kind of pale," Destiny said.

"Yes, I'm fine. That tuna salad I had earlier is doing a number on me," I lied.

"Well, that was your last appointment for the day, because your four o'clock appointment cancelled. We can call it a day, unless you have something else you wanted to do."

"Well you can head on home. I'ma stay behind and go over some files. I got court in the morning and I want to be prepared."

"Okay, babe. I've got to get Amaiya from her program. I'll see you later."I locked the door after Destiny left. I walked back to my office, waited about twenty minutes, and left.

I banged on the door repeatedly. "Open the fucking door!" I yelled.

This was one time I didn't give a fuck if one of those nosey bitches were around. Imani opened the door looking at me with a lot of attitude. I stormed past her.

"My son is studying. Don't come up in here with this bullshit."

"Bullshit! After that stunt you pulled today? How dare you come up in my office like that? Yo, sit down B! What is your problem?" I asked.

"Problem? I don't have one. See, you underestimate me. You think because I ain't got no college degree or have money like your bitch, you can just run over me. Well this shit is over with. Either you do right or I promise you'll regret fucking me and my son over."

"Yo, you're one stupid chick. I keep telling you I love you. Why don't you see that, huh? Everything I do is for you and my son. Why is that so hard to believe!" I yelled and hit the wall, punching a fist-sized hole in it.

"Don't come in here putting holes in my shit."

"Man, whatever! I'll pay for this shit."

"You know what Hassan? That's your problem. You think you can come up here and always use money to fix everything, but it don't always work like that. My son and I have fucking feelings."

"You think feelings pay these fucking bills? You think feelings keep a roof over your head or buy the car you driving? Hell no, you need money for this shit!" I yelled. I was pissed the fuck off.

She stood there with her arms crossed, gritting on me. This bitch was pissing me off. I loved her ass, but she was making it difficult for me. There was no way I was going to let her get in the way of me living the good life. It pisses me off that she was too dumb to realize that we were on our way to the top. All this bullshit she was doing was irrelevant. Imani needed to realize I was no longer the hood nigga but a lawyer with clients. I couldn't afford to be caught up in domestic drama.

I turned away and opened the door; if I hung around, I had a feeling I might beat her ass.

"So you just going to leave like that?"

"B, what the hell you want from me?" I closed the door and turned around to face her.

I knew what she was begging for and as bad as I didn't want to because of the stunt she pulled, I had no choice but to oblige. At least I knew I could calm her down a little. I stepped toward her.

"I know why you acting like this. You need daddy to beat that pussy up." I put on my sex appeal.

"Whatever." She smacked her lips together.

I grabbed her aggressively and pushed her onto the couch. I got behind her, pulling her pants and drawers down. I took out my dick that had instantly gotten hard and rubbed it against her pussy lips. I then entered her with force. I held her hips and sank deeper into her slippery pussy.

"*Aargh*," she groaned and moaned with excitement.

"Take this dick, bitch! It's all yours." I continued to pound her walls harder.

The more she moaned, the more excited I got. I felt my veins enlarging and my dick started to throb.

"*Aarghhhhhhhhh*," I groaned out as I busted all up in her.

My knees buckled underneath me and I fell on the couch. I lay there a few minutes and then it really hit me; Destiny was expecting me home for dinner. I got up and rushed into the bathroom to wash off my dick with soap and water. I kissed her on the cheek and hastily left the apartment.

CHAPTER THIRTEEN

Destiny Clarke

A woman's intuition is everything and shouldn't be second-guessed. I knew I could get overzealous sometimes and act off impulse, but today it was my intuition—something was wrong. It started right after that new secretary arrived at the office. Hassan's behavior changed and he seemed a bit nervous and edgy. I had no idea what was wrong, but I made a mental note to pay close attention.

I understood that Hassan was a fine brother that was making a few dollars and bitches were attracted to a man who seemed to have his shit together. The thing is, I'm in the picture and I'll be damned if any one of these lazy bitches was going to walk off the street, come up in here, and benefit off of something that I helped build. I was my husband's keeper and a bitch has to go through me to get to his money.

When I questioned if he was all right, he told me some bullshit about some tuna he ate. The nigga must've forgotten I made his lunch and it was baked chicken today. I also sensed he was lying when he told me he was going to stay behind. I didn't object. Instead I kissed him, gathered my stuff and walked out of the office.

I took the elevator down to the parking deck, got in my car, and sat waiting. I hoped I was wrong. I watched as he walked to his car and pulled out. I waited a few seconds, and then I pulled off too. I managed to keep a

safe distance so he wouldn't spot my car. As he got off the
parkway, I noticed he was going the opposite direction of
our home. "What are you up to?" I whispered to myself. I
managed to stay back, until he turned on Chester Avenue.
I slowed down as he pulled into the driveway. He got out
of his car and banged on the door like a lunatic. This fool
didn't bother to look around to check his surroundings;
if he had, he would have seen my black car. I watched as
a woman opened the door and he walked into the house,
but I couldn't make out the woman's face from where I
was parked.

My heart started beating quickly and as I gripped my
steering wheel, I wanted to know who that woman was
or why was my husband at her home. Everything in me
was screaming for me to go knock on the door, until my
telephone interrupted my thoughts. I looked and saw
that it was Amaiya's school. Damn! I totally forgot I was
supposed to pick her up. The clock in the car read 4:40
p.m. and I should have been there half an hour ago.

I answered the phone and didn't wait for a response.

"I'm sorry, I'm on the way."

I put on my seatbelt and sped off. I was slipping on
my parental duties. I'd never been late before to pick my
child up, and I pressed on the gas all the way to White
Plains Road. I honked my horn at some old fool who was
holding up traffic.

"Get your old ass out of the street!" I yelled.

"Go fuck yourself!" he shot back at me.

I gave him the middle finger and backed up so I could
go around his ass. This old bastard had no idea this was
not the day to fuck with me.

When I pulled up at the school, I saw her standing in
the front office.

"Ma, you're late," she screamed

"Hello there, Mrs. Clarke. I was kind of worried because you are never late picking her up."

"I apologize. I was working in the city today and traffic was jammed up."

"No worries. I know how bad the traffic can get."

"Come on, let's go home. "

"Thanks again, Ms. Balas."

"Alright, Amaiya. I'll see you tomorrow," she said.

I held my daughter's hand and we walked out to my car. No matter what I was going through, she always managed to brighten up my day.

I still couldn't get Hassan off my mind. Just when I thought we were on the right path, this happened. I picked up my phone and checked to see if he'd called while I was in the school, but there were no missed calls. I dialed his phone and it went straight to voicemail.

"Mommy, where's Daddy?"

"Your daddy is working late. He'll be home in a little while."

We got home and I made Amaiya macaroni and cheese, her favorite meal. I changed my mind about cooking for Hassan and myself since I'd lost my appetite. I was tired and needed to take a bath so I could relax a little.

"Mommy, is you okay?"

"Yes, I'm just tired. Now go get in your bed and watch TV."

"Okay. Love you Mommy." She kissed me and gave me a quick hug.

I burst out crying. I sat on my bed with my head buried in my hands. My chest tightened up on me because of how hard I was crying inside. I heard the garage door and I knew he was home. I ran to the bathroom and washed my face. I was wiping my face when he walked into the room.

"Hey babe."

I didn't respond. Instead, I walked to my bed.

"You all right? I thought you said you was coming home to cook. I'm starved."

"Yeah, well, I changed my mind. Did you get all your work done at the office?"

"Yes I did. I'm all set for tomorrow."

"Really? I called your cell and the office phone, but you didn't pick up."

"You know me babe, when I'm deep into a case, I don't answer the phone."

"Really? That's news to me."

"Damn, Destiny! You know I was working. What's up with all this attitude?"

"Attitude from me? I don't have a attitude. You know Hassan, a man only lies to his wife when he has something to hide. So that leaves me to wonder what you're hiding,"

"Destiny, here you go again, accusing me of doing things. I told you I had to go over a case and that's what I did. Nothing more, nothing less!" he yelled.

I didn't back down. This dumbass man thought I didn't know what I was talking about.

"Baby, listen, I'm not cheating on you. I gave you my word last time and I meant it. I'm not going to risk losing you."

"So tell me, if you're so truthful, why did you lie and say you were at the office?"

"Destiny, I swear on my mama, I ain't lying, I was going over a case!"

I saw that he wasn't going to give in and as much as I wanted to confront him, I quickly decided not to. I needed to find out who lived at that address without him knowing I was on to him.

Hassan Clarke

Money was flowing. My partner and I, along with the firm, were doing really well. Who would've ever thought that I would be an attorney, and a damn good one at that? I also noticed that the more money I made, the more bitches started throwing themselves at me. It was funny how the tables had turned; back in the day they would have never given me the time of day, but now they were all up in my face. It was all good because I was fucking almost every day of the week.

My business life was good, but my personal life was in disarray. Hiring Imani was not a brilliant idea. She kept an eye on me, especially when the clients were female. The rest of the time, she was in my office. Whenever I was in the office trying to go over a case or just enjoying a little bit of free time, she would bust through the door. Most times, before I could say anything, she would start taking off her drawers. I couldn't resist, especially when she showed me that pretty pussy. I don't know what it was, but she got my mind fucked all the way up.

After I while, I managed to keep everything on the low. I saw how my partner and the paralegal would look at me after Imani walked out of my office. Shit really got serious when my partner confronted me.

"Let me talk to you real quick," my partner Leon said to me

I followed him into his office and closed the door.

"What's good, you aiight?"

"Listen bro, you know you're my ace and we make a good team."

"Yeah, so what's going on?"

"You need to cut shorty loose."

"Who you talking about, the secretary?"

"Yes, that's exactly who I'm talking about. I don't want to be all up in your business, but it's obvious what is going on between y'all."

"Going on between us? Ain't nothing going on between us. Dog, you trippin'." I nervously laughed.

"Am I? I see how she looks at you and y'all have all those long meetings in your office. Come on, even Ray Charles can see that y'all are fooling around."

"Yo, my man, I'm married and I love my wife. I don't know what you're seeing, but you're wrong buddy."

"Okay, if you say so. Just be careful because this could get messy. Don't forget you're running a firm that relies on integrity and trust."

"I know. I'm running a business, remember? I started the firm," I said, before I walked out of his office.

"Hassan—"

"Not now," I cut Imani off.

I walked into my office and locked the door, sat in my chair and loosened my tie. I felt like I was suffocating. I leaned back and closed my eyes. I knew I was wrong for snapping on my partner. I don't know if I was angry that he was spitting some real shit or because people knew I was fucking around with the secretary. I knew the way I was living was foul and needed to change. I let out a long sigh. I was in such a mess and I had no idea how to get out of it. I loved having all these bitches, but I knew that it was only a matter of time before all this shit hit the fan.

Destiny Clarke

Our ten-year anniversary was approaching and we decided to renew our vows. I took control this time and put my foot down; I didn't want his family there, especially his old, gorilla-looking mother. I planned to have a small ceremony with my mom, my best friend, and a few of my coworkers. Then we planned to take a two-week cruise to the Caribbean. I was looking forward to taking a well-deserved vacation.

It was my night to work. God knows I was getting tired of working the night shift. I'd been saying for years that I was going to switch to the day shift. I was tired and I wanted to be in my bed at night with my husband like every other woman. I was about to go on my lunch break at 1:00 a.m, when my phone started to ring. I looked at the caller ID and it was an unknown caller. I picked it up.

"Hello?" No one answered.

"Hello?" I said again, this time with an attitude.

There was still no answer. I quickly hung up my phone.

"Everything all right?" one of the nurses asked me.

"Yes, I guess. Somebody called me and just sat on the line."

"Somebody got a secret crush. Maybe he got cold feet," she joked.

"Yeah right, I only have eyes for the wonderful Mr. Clarke. . . ." before I could finish my sentence, the phone rang again from the same unknown number. I picked up again and still no answer. It continued ringing until I finally got fed up and cut the phone off. This was some strange shit because I had no idea who would be playing on my damn phone this time of night.

Soon as I got home, I went to confront Hassan. I wanted to know if he gave anyone my phone number. He denied doing such a thing and told me to change my number. The harassing calls continued for days. Whoever it was would just sit on the phone, breathing. The calls got so bad; I would have to cut off my phone while I was at work.

I couldn't take it anymore. One morning after work, I drove to the Sprint shop and got my number changed. I gave my new number only to my mama, Hassan, Amaiya's school, and my girlfriend.

***

Speaking of girlfriend, it'd been a minute since she and I chilled out. She and I were best friends, but because of our hectic lives, we barely had time to chop it up like we used to. I hadn't seen her in over a year, which was bad.

"Hello."

"Hey stranger, how you been?"

"I'm good, trying to work and take care of business."

"I hear you chica, are you still at the hospital?"

"Girl, yes, you know that's my second home. It ain't been the same since you left though."

"I prefer Lady of Mercy Hospital. Westchester Medical was working us too damn hard. I couldn't take it no more, and that damn head nurse was a bitch."

"Child, yes, she is on day shift now. We have a new head nurse and she don't be trippin' like that. We also have a couple of new ladies on the floor."

"Anyways, enough about the job. What's going on with you, how my god baby doing?"

"Girl, she's fine. Growing up fast. She keeps asking for her auntie. She wants to come to your house."

"You know what? I'm off this weekend. I'ma come get her, so we can spend some time together."

"She'll love it and I'll get a break. God knows I love that child, but she's a handful."

"Yeah, that's why I decided I don't want no children. I've got Sasha, she's enough."

Sasha was the dog, but if you didn't know better, you would think Sasha was a baby from the way she talked about her.

"So how is married life treating you? Miss 'I-will-never-get-married.'"

I wanted to lie to my girl and tell her everything was great, but I paused.

"Des, what's wrong? You and Hassan cool, right?"

"Girl, I don't know what's going on. I ain't got no proof, but my gut is telling me he's cheating. The other day I followed him and he went in some bitch's house and lied to me that he was at work."

"His ass better not be playing considering how much you do for his ass. That's what is wrong with these dudes—they don't ever do right by a good woman, but are quick to wife these old, raggedy-ass hoes."

"Girl, I ain't goin' front. I'm fucked up about it because I busted my ass to help this nigga when his own fuck ass family wouldn't help him. I'm just hurting for real."

"I feel you, but you know what though, if that nigga is cheating on you, he deserve to get his head bust wide open."

"I'm not goin' say shit, because I'm too pissed off. One thing I know is that I'm done being anybody's fool."

"Girl, these niggas ain't loyal. You can only use them for dick and money. All that 'I love you' shit is fake."

My phone started to beep; it was Mama.

"All right chick, that's Mama. I'll call you Friday," I said, before I clicked over.

"Hey Mama, how you doing?"

"Not too good. My head is bothering me again."

"Did you take something for it?"

"No, not as yet. I called to see if you found a place for the reception?"

I took a long pause before I responded. "Mama there won't be any reception," I squeezed out.

"What you mean? I told you I'd pay for it."

"Mama, stop! We won't be renewing our vows. I need to be looking for a divorce attorney instead."

"Are you serious? What done happened now? A few days ago you were excited about renewing your vows and now this. . . ."

"Mama, I don't want to talk about it. Just know that it ain't happening."

"Okay baby, you know Mama love you and if you need to come here, you know you and Amaiya will always have a home."

"Thank you, Mama, and I love you too, but it's my damn house and if anybody leaving, it's not goin' be me."

"All right honey. I'm not goin' hold you up much longer. Kiss my grandbaby for me and tell her nana loves her."

"All right Mama, get some rest and call me if you need me."

CHAPTER FOURTEEN

Imani Gibson

What was supposed to be a few months turned into years; every time I asked Hassan about him leaving that bitch, he kept on telling me he just needed a little more time. My baby had grown up and here his mama was, still playing house with his daddy.

I was getting restless and felt Hassan had had enough time. I was ready to let the bitch know what had been going on. Hassan was my man and the father of my son. I wanted her to know he didn't love her and the reason he was with her was because she had some money. I recalled when I first met her. I examined her from head to toe and saw nothing special about her ass. She was just a regular ass ho with money; she didn't seem like anything Hassan would've fucked with. She was no competition for me. I hate to brag, but I had a badass shape, small waist, and round fat ass. Every nigga was looking to wife a chick like me and here my dumb ass was, chasing a nigga that couldn't get his shit together.

"We getting off early today," Hassan said as he walked over to my desk.

"Why, what's going on?" I asked.

"You said you wanted a new ride. How about we go car shopping?"

"Are you serious?"

"Either you want it or you don't."

"Hell yeah I want it," I confirmed.

By 3:30 p.m., Hassan and I left out in his car. I felt good; it's about time he stepped up and started spending some real paper on me. After all, I kept his dick satisfied.

My eyes popped open as he pulled into a Lexus car dealer's parking lot. This has to be a joke, I thought to myself. There's no way he was about to cop me a fucking Lexus.

"Stay right here," he said and walked off to talk to a car salesman.

I glanced around; there were so many nice cars, I knew it was going to be hard for me to decide. Minutes later, Hassan returned. "Let's walk around so you can pick which car you want."

"Are you fucking serious?" I didn't wait for an answer. I jumped on him and gave him a big wet one.

"Yo, chill! We are out in public." He pushed me off.

Any other time I would have reacted, but not this time; I was too goddamn happy that I could finally get rid of that hoopty that I had. Yes Lord, these bitches couldn't say shit to me now. We walked through the long rows of cars, and I felt so confused until a red 2012 Lexus RX 350 caught my attention. I stopped and peeped inside. I noticed the brand new leather and the spacious foot room. I instantly fell in love.

"This one! I need to test drive this one," I yelled out with excitement.

"You hear the lady," Hassan said to the car salesman.

Hassan handled the paperwork while I took my new ride on the road. I felt like new money. I never thought sucking and riding dick could get me the finer things in life. I hit the highway and back. I loved that I wasn't sitting low anymore and the car was fast. Everything was worked out and five hours later, I drove off in a brand new Lexus crossover.

Hassan said he had a meeting and had to go. I was cool because I planned to drop by his mom's house. When I pulled up, his sister and one of her friends was sitting outside the building. I parked and jumped out.

"Hey y'all."

"Bitch, I was wondering who this was. Whose ride you borrowed?"

"No honey. I'm the owner of this nice machine." I bragged and dangled the keys.

"Bitch, whatever! Just the other day your ass was broke and now you come around here talking about you own this whip. Quit stunting," Charmaine said.

"Well, hmm. . . I'ma never be broke as long as I got pussy and this here is a generous gift, courtesy of your brother." I wish I could have taken a picture of her face. I don't know if it was jealousy or if she was shocked.

"Damn bitch. In that case, I must say you a bad bitch. You must be doing something right for my brother to go all out like that."

"Maybe he's just growing up and he's realizing that I'm his woman and I deserve nothing but the best."

"Yeah, whatever." We all busted out laughing.

To a stranger, it might seem like we were arguing, but nah, that's how we often got down.

They got in and we went to Bay Plaza to chill a little and I dropped them off afterwards. It was getting late and Josiah was home, maybe wondering where I was. I couldn't wait to see his face when he saw Mommy's new car.

Destiny Clarke

After all these years, I thought Hassan would finally get his act together. I held off on the divorce, because the truth was I hated to fail and getting a divorce was the ultimate failure. Some days were better than others. Whenever he was in his sweet mood, he would shower me with gifts and tell me a million times, how much he loved me. Other days he was just as mean as a drunk was, but he was worse, because he wasn't even drinking.

It was 11:17 p.m. I knew because I'd been checking the time back to back. Hassan didn't come home after work and when I called his phone, it kept going to voicemail. I left him several messages, but still didn't hear from him. I couldn't sleep, because I knew he was up to no-good again. I was hurting so bad I started to cry. I was mentally tired and physically drained. I got up, went downstairs, and started to pour a glass of his vodka. I needed something strong to help me ease the pain. I didn't bother to get a glass; I put the bottle to my head. The strong liquor left a burning sensation in my chest, but it didn't stop me from taking another swig from the bottle. "Damn you, Hassan," I screamed.

I threw the bottle into the wall. The broken pieces shattered all over the wall, then onto the floor. I got up off the stool and staggered into my living room. I laid across the sofa, indulging in my misery. My thoughts were no longer clear and I felt the walls around me spinning. I held my head and screamed, "Oh my God, help me." Those were the last words I said before I passed out.

"Mommy, Mommy, wake up," I heard Amaiya yell.

The sound from her squeaky voice triggered a terrible headache. I opened my eyes to see my princess pouting.

"Mommy, I'm late."

"What time is it?" I managed to sit up.

"It's after eight and I was supposed to be at school an hour ago. I tried calling Daddy and he didn't pick up."

"I'm sorry, baby. Let me wash my face and I'll be ready."

This little girl acts like she's the mother and I'm the child, I thought. I washed my face, made a cup of coffee, and headed out the door. I was in no shape to drive, but I had no choice but to drop her off. I also noticed his ass didn't make it home. Tears started to gather in my eyes, but I quickly caught myself. I didn't want my child to see me crying.

"Okay honey, have a good day. I love you too."

"Love you too, Mommy. Don't forget I've got basketball practice this evening."

"I won't forget you. I'll be there." I assured her.

I watched as she walked up the stairs and disappeared into the school. *My little girl has grown up*, I thought as I pulled off.

I dialed Hassan's phone and it was still turned off. This was serious. In all the years that we'd been together, he had never spent an entire night away from home. I'm not counting the time that I put him out. It's damn well into the next day and he hadn't called or shown up.

I made a U-turn and headed to my Mom's house. I was feeling distraught, my head was pounding, and I was hungry, but food was the last thing on my mind.

I dialed Mama's number.

"Hello dear."

"Open the door. I'm pullin' up in a minute."

I parked my car into the driveway, grabbed my pocketbook, and got out of the car. Mama was standing in the doorway with her hands akimbo. I walked in and she followed behind.

"I was making breakfast and coffee. Did you eat?"

"No, I'm not hungry, but I will take a cup of coffee."

I sat on the stool in the kitchen, watching her as she scrambled eggs. I sure missed those days when she used to make me breakfast, especially when it used to be her and me. Those days were long gone and now I had my own little princess to cook for.

"Here you go honey." She placed a cup of coffee in front of me.

"Thanks Mama."

"I'm worried about you. You look like you ain't been to sleep. Is everything alright?"

"Mama, it's Hassan. He didn't come home last night."

She took a seat beside me and put her hand on mine.

"Oh baby, I'm sorry. Did you call him?" she questioned.

"Yes, the last time I talked to him was yesterday around eleven a.m. I thought he'd be home around five p.m. He didn't come then, so I started calling him and his phone kept going to voicemail. . . . " my voice trailed off.

"Oh Lord. You think something happened to him?"

"Mama, trust me—if something did happen to him, I'd be the first person they'd call."

"Destiny, I don't want to intrude, but do you think Hassan has been seeing another woman?"

"Mama I ain't got no proof, but I feel in my heart that's what it is. Where could a married man be all night and all morning?" I shook my head in disgust.

She squeezed my hand and spoke, "I know you love him, but if you stay with him, it's not going to change. You need to dig deep into your soul, find your strength, and get out of it. You hear me? You're too good of a woman to keep putting up with this bullshit."

"I know, but I put so much into this relationship, both emotionally and financially. I helped build that firm from the ground up. How do I walk away from all that? And for another woman to reap the benefits of my sweat. I built that Mama!" I yelled in frustration.

I saw a tear fall from her eyes. She took her glasses off and placed them on the counter.

"You know, the day I got you from that group home, I looked at you and I made a promise to myself that I was going to take care of you by any means necessary. If anybody hurt you, I was going to kill them. When I found out that bastard was raping you right under my nose, I wanted to hurt him bad, but it was too late then because the police already had him. I might not have pushed you out of me, but you're my child. I don't like to see you hurting and I can't do anything about it. Here you're hurting again behind another no-good ass boy. He don't deserve the title of 'man.' I want to hurt him bad, but that wouldn't do any good. You need to talk to a divorce lawyer soon, but before you do, you need a private investigator. A good damn one that could dig up all the dirt that bastard been hiding."

I sat there, crying and listening to Mama. She made it seem so easy, but this was my life and I had no idea how to pick up the pieces of my shattered soul.

CHAPTER FIFTEEN

Imani Gibson

I was sick and tired of being the other woman. I'm not sure which part of that Hassan didn't get. I had to admit that our relationship had gotten better after I started working at the firm. As far as us fooling around in his office, things had changed. Hassan wanted to keep it professional because his business partner was on to us; he mentioned it wouldn't be a good look for a married man to be having an extramarital affair. I played it cool because my eyes were set on the top spot.

Even though I didn't say much, I was getting tired of all his promises of leaving her. Loneliness was kicking in, especially at night when I was in bed by myself. Some nights, I couldn't sleep. I would lay in bed restless, wondering if she was sucking and fucking him as well as I did. A few times, I got in my car and drove over to their house. I would sit outside listening to slow jams and crying my heart out.

The music was blasting through my Bose surround system as I cleaned my apartment from head to toe. I also had neck bones, greens, and rice on the stove. I was making my man his favorite meal. "Ha ha," I chuckled to myself. I remember him saying that bitch didn't know how to cook. Her ass knew she was wrong; you had to know how to fuck him good, suck him good, and feed him good.

Josiah had gone to his grandma's for the night, so it was just the two of us. I took a shower and put on my little red Victoria Secret's two-piece and a pair of heels. I planned on having him for the entire night. Fuck him going home to that bitch.

He called and said he was on the way. I lit the candles and placed two glasses of wine on the table. I then made his plate. When I opened the door for him, I saw his eyes pop open. He stood there staring, mouth wide open.

"Hello, come on in," I joked.

"Damn B, you fucking with a nigga hard as hell, right now."

"Chill out, babe. Wash your hands and come eat your dinner. I made your favorite." I pulled on his tie and pulled him toward me, placing a big wet one on his lips.

He grabbed my ass, but I wiggled away.

"Come on, the food gonna be cold." I smiled.

We sat down at the table, eating, laughing, and talking like old times when it was only the two of us. I looked as he stared at me.

"What's wrong?"

"Nothing. Just thinking."

"Thinking about what?"

"Me, you, and our future." He took a sip of his wine.

"Really?" I side-eyed him.

"Yeah, I mean you been riding with me for a minute now and I know I ain't been the best, but you stuck around and still make me happy. I 'ont say it a lot, but I appreciate you and I want to take our relationship to the next level."

"Next level?" What was this nigga talking about? He was married, so there was no next level. I didn't respond. Instead, I sat there looking at him. He reached over and took my hand.

"Listen B, I'm about to divorce Destiny. I'm in the process of getting all my finances secure, so she can't get shit in the divorce. I don't even want to give her alimony. I know they goin' get me for child support and that's cool. I need about another three months and it's a wrap. I'm telling you this, 'cause I need you to quit the firm and chill out while I handle everything."

"You want me to quit? It ain't like they know it's me."

"I understand, but things could get sticky and I don't want you involved in it. "

"So when I'm supposed to be quitting?"

"In another week, so we can hire someone else."

"Aiight," I said reluctantly.

"Listen, I'm not bullshitting you. This week coming up, I want you to start looking for a four-bedroom house out in the White Plains area. Something you like."

"You fucking playing right?" I yelled.

"Man, chill out. You want to move out of this piece of shit, right?"

"I love you, Hassan. I love you." I started to cry.

Growing up in the hood, the only thing I'd ever wanted to do was move out to the suburbs. Now I could get my son into a better school. The tears continued flowing, but this time they were tears of joy.

We ended the evening with a second glass of wine, which I'd made especially for him. Like I said earlier, he was not making it home to the Misses tonight.

"Damn, it's like all my energy drained out of my body," he said as he got up and walked over to the couch.

"Lie down babe. Get some rest."

"I'm going to take a quick nap. Wake me up in an hour, I gotta make it home."

Not tonight, I thought.

"Sure, I got you," I replied.

He tried to say something, but he was gone before he could finish the sentence. I went to the bedroom to get him a blanket. I took off his shoes and covered him up.

After I finished cleaning the kitchen and mopping the floor, I went to check on him; he was fast asleep. That sleeping pill did wonders on him, I thought. I checked his jacket pocket and pulled his phone out.

After I got into my room, I locked my door and got into my bed. I cut the phone on and started searching. The first thing I saw was a couple texts from a chick named Tanya. I read the back and forth text messages and I realized that he was fucking her too. Really? Here I was, faithful to this nigga and not only did he get married on me, but he also had another bitch. According to the text, he was with her two days ago. I was too upset after I finished reading the messages, I wanted to go in there and confront him, but a voice in my head warned, *bitch you trippin', this nigga just offered to buy you a house and you tripping over some bitch, he's only fucking.* I also saw a few messages from his wife.

Where are you? I'm trying to reach you.

This is one lonely bitch, tonight, I thought and smiled.

I dialed Tanya's number from his phone. She didn't pick up at first, but she called right back. "Hey babe."

"Hello. Surprise."

"Who is this and why're you using Hassan's phone?"

"Listen to me bitch: I'm Imani and I'm his woman. So who are you?"

"If you have his phone, then you know exactly who I am," this little bitch said.

I wanted to jump through the phone and rip her fucking head off.

"You know what, I ain't goin' argue with you, but if I ever see you I'm going to beat yo' ass, you little bitch. "

"Ha ha! You're too funny. Why are you on the phone arguing over another woman's husband? See, you are one dumb bitch. At least the wife has more class," she said, then hung the phone up.

I tried calling back, but the bitch had her phone turned off. Whew, I was too mad. These bitches had no idea who they were playing with. I guessed I had to show them.

Hassan Clarke

I was ready to hang up my player's robe and settle down with my woman. I wasn't getting any younger and I felt like it was time for me to sit back and live life a little better. I had money in the bank and over the summer I bought a boat and I was ready to sail to different parts of the world. Who would've thought a dude like me would be living like this? I even paid down on a house for my mama. I was happy that I was able to help out my family. Being the only son and also the oldest child, I had to step up to the plate and make it happen.

I'd also been banking money in the Cayman Islands in various accounts. Destiny only knew about the one account that we shared and I wanted to keep it that way. I'd been planning my great escape; I was tired of being married to her. Truthfully, the love wasn't there anymore. Fucking her was like screwing a dead log—no bit of excitement. Lately, when I was home, I would go into the bathroom, log onto one of those porn sites and beat my dick off. I wasn't too pressed for that dry pussy. Furthermore, her ass had been actin' stupid. Kept on asking me a million and one questions; I swore the other day she was on to me when I told her I was at the office. I'm trying to be wicked, I tried to love her, but her attitude was too much for me and my family couldn't stand her. It was fucked up that I couldn't invite my mama to the crib because of how Destiny treated her.

Imani on the other hand, was the total opposite. She was my mother's favorite. Lately, my love for her has grown stronger. She hardly fussed anymore and her sex was always on point. I never thought I would ever say this, but I was wide open over shorty and my relationship with my son has gotten better too. I didn't care if Destiny found out about him; I was done neglecting my seed. She had to know the truth one day, but right now I was buying time.

CHAPTER SIXTEEN

Destiny Clarke

Things definitely took a turn for the worse over the last few months. The disappearing acts became too extreme. Last week, he stayed out three nights straight. When I confronted him, he lied. Claimed he was at his partner's house playing cards and fell asleep. And the nights he was home, his phone constantly rang. He would look at the caller ID, and then cut the phone off. One night, after I saw what he did, I asked who was calling so late. He told me it was his sister. I didn't say a word. I rolled over and closed my eyes.

I was up early. I had an appointment with a prominent private investigator. Word on the street was he was one of the best; he could find out anything or anyone who was hiding. I couldn't believe I let my mother talk me into doing this, but the truth was I needed to know.

I was dressed in black pants with a pair of Steve Madden stilettos. I had my hair wrapped up in a bun. It'd been months since the last time I got dressed up. I was in a great mood this morning. I had K. Michelle's song "Can't Raise a Man," blasting through my speakers. The words of that song seemed as if she were sending a message directly to me. I felt tears well up in my eyes, but I used force and pushed them back. I wasn't going to cry. Besides, I didn't want to smear my make-up.

I pulled up at the office on White Plains Road and parked. I strutted to the door, rang the bell, and I was immediately buzzed in. I walked in and stood in a trance. I was expecting a fat, burly-looking man; at least that's how PI's looked on the television. Not in this case. Mr. Spencer was a tall, dark-skinned brother with muscles that made me want to say, "Can I touch?"

"Hello, you must be Mrs. Clarke." He extended his hand.

"Yes, that's me. You must be Mr. Spencer."

"Yes, you got that right. Please take a seat." He pointed to the chair.

"Thank you," I said and then sat across from him.

"So tell me, what brings you to my side of the hood?"

"Well, Mr. Spencer, I've been married for over ten years and I think my husband is stepping out on me. I want to file for divorce, but my husband has money and a firm that I helped build. All I want is proof that he's an adulterer so I can take this into the courts."

"I understand. I always tell my clients that I might find something that could hurt them. Sometimes it's best just to leave, instead of digging for dirt."

"Mr. Spencer, I mean no disrespect, but I'm a grown ass woman and I can handle whatever you may find. I'm not here to waste your time. I want proof," I said in a fierce tone

"Okay ma'am, you're the boss and I hear you loud and clear."

I gave him details of things that seemed suspicious. I also gave him the address of the woman's house that I'd followed Hassan to. I gave him every piece of information that I thought was relevant, and a recent picture of Hassan.

"Okay Mrs. Clarke. I'll be in touch soon."

"Alright, thank you for everything Mr. Spencer." I got up, put on my sunglasses and walked out of the office. I held my head high and smiled. I was so over this bullshit and I was ready to take control.

The anticipation of waiting on Mr. Spencer was killing me. I pretended nothing was wrong when I was around Hassan. I had no idea what he was up to, but I was getting a bad vibe from him, so I kept my distance. I stayed busy working and caring for Amaiya.

It was my day off, so I decided to do some laundry before I picked up Amaiya. I picked up a pair of Hassan's pants to put into the washer. I emptied his pockets out and there was a piece of paper inside of one of the pockets; I took it out and placed it on top of the dryer. After I finished loading the machine, I glanced at the paper on my way out, so I turned and grabbed it up. When I opened it up, I saw it was a receipt from a Lexus car dealership for a vehicle that was purchased two months ago. Two months ago? I asked myself.

I didn't get a Lexus and he didn't get one, so who got a Lexus? There was only one way to find out. I slipped into an Aeropostale sweat suit, grabbed my bag and ran out the door. It was one thing to be cheating, but it was a whole different ball game when you're tricking on these hoes. A fucking Lexus? That bitch's pussy better be made of platinum. I did 80 mph all the way into the city. I didn't have time to worry about getting pulled over. I was going to confront this man. I had enough. I didn't care if it was his place of business. Shit, my name may not be on the paper, but my money damn sure built it.

I saw the secretary at the desk and she shot me a dirty look when I walked in.

"Is my husband in?"

"He's in a meeting, you can't just barge in there," she said, before I pushed the door and entered his office.

There were a woman and a man sitting in the chair across from him.

"Honey, I'm in the middle of a meeting."

"Meeting is over. Please excuse yourselves." I looked at both of them.

"Destiny, what are you doing? I'm in the middle of going over a case with them."

"Like I said before, this meeting is over!" I yelled.

The couple got up without saying another word and stormed out, closing the door behind them. "What in God's name are you doing, coming up in here like you fucking crazy," he said with rage in his voice.

"I don't give a damn about you or this fucking business. What I want to know is when did you buy a Lexus and who did you buy it for, huh?"

"Lower your voice. I don't know what you're talking about."

"Really? You had this in your pocket." I threw the paper in his face.

He grabbed it, read it and smiled.

"Oh, this is what you're tripping about? My homeboy Corey asked me to co-sign this vehicle for him. I forgot I had the receipt in my pocket, I was supposed to give it to him."

"You know what Hassan, you're a fucking liar. Unless you fucking Corey, there's no way you bought him a fucking, brand new Lexus. I want you to know, I'm on to you. I swear you going to pay for all the shit you put me through."

"Destiny, baby, calm down! I swear on my mama, that's Corey's car and I'm not doing anything to hurt you. You're my wife and I love you." He tried to touch me.

"Don't you fucking touch me, you hear me?" I stormed out of the office.

I walked up to the secretary. "Listen to me: don't you ever tell me when I can go into my husband's office. You're nothing but the help, so please act accordingly before I get your ass out of here."

"Lady, something is wrong with you."

"You heard what I said."

I didn't wait to hear what that heffer had to say, so I walked off on her ass.

Imani Gibson

After all the chaos that happened at the job earlier, I was in no mood to talk to Hassan, so I left early. I stopped by the bodega on the corner of East 228th Street and White Plains Road to pick up some milk and snacks for Josiah. On the way out, I ran into Corey. I hadn't seen this dude in years, since our last rendezvous.

"Damn shorty, what's good?" He walked up on me.

"Hey Corey. How you doing?" I tried to play it off.

"Damn, I tried calling you a few times, but you ain't answer."

"Yeah, I've been busy; plus me and Hassan trying to work on our relationship."

"Fuck that nigga; he used to be one of us, but since he a lawyer now, he act like he 'ont fuck with the crew no more."

"I don't think it's like that; he just really busy, you know?"

"Enough about that dude. Let's talk 'bout us. So tell me: when are you going to let this nigga know he ain't the daddy? I mean, I've been patiently playing the back seat for a minute now, but the other day I see my li'l man and he the spitting image of me. Shit, he need to know who his daddy really is."

"Corey, come on. We talked about this and you agreed you're in no position to take care of a child."

"I don't give a fuck about what we talked about. That was when he was born. I got my shit together now. I got my own crib and a good job at the body shop in Mount Vernon. I just want to be a part of my son's life."

I saw the desperation in his eyes. I knew I had to do something fast. I couldn't risk him fucking up things for me.

"Do you want to chill at the house for a little while? Maybe we can talk a little more about this."

"Bet, I'm parked over there. I'll follow you." He pointed to an old, beat up Toyota Camry.

My head started spinning. I wished like hell I hadn't run into this fool. I mean, I know I fucked up when I gave him the pussy. I was only trying to get back at Hassan for some shit he did to me and what better way to do that than to fuck his right-hand man. The first time we slept together, we were both fucked up off Xanax and weed. After that, this fool kept blackmailing me to sleep with him and if I didn't, he threatened to go to Hassan. This was something I couldn't risk.

A month after we had sex, I found out that I was pregnant. I panicked. I didn't know what to do because I had forgiven Hassan and we were back together again. I had to act fast. I had sex with Hassan and waited a few weeks, then I told him I was pregnant. At first, Hassan doubted that I was pregnant by him, but after a little convincing, he happily accepted Josiah.

I had to beg Corey to stay quiet about the baby and he agreed. It only made sense because at the time he was in no position financially to support a baby. For years, I prayed that he would leave it alone and luckily, he did for a while. I was too happy when Hassan left the streets alone and stopped hanging around Corey and his crew.

***

Shit always fucked you up when you were on the right path. *Why did I have to run into this fool?* I parked in my spot and he parked beside me.

"Damn B, you driving in style. Who bought you that Lexus?"

"Hassan bought it for me," I said in an annoyed tone.

"Shit, that nigga making money now. No wonder he 'ont fuck with a nigga no more. I thought he got married."

"Yes, he's married, but he's about to get a divorce."

"Damn, that pussy got that nigga like that. I always told you, you got that ole sugar pussy." He grinned.

"Do you want something to drink?"

"Yeah, something strong."

I poured him a little of Hassan's vodka. I handed him the cup, then sat beside him. I started rubbing his leg.

"Damn Ma, you missing a nigga, huh?"

I didn't say a word. I just smiled and kept rubbing toward his crotch. God knew I didn't want to go there with his fool, but I had no choice. I needed him to keep his mouth shut until I got the house and Hassan got his divorce. I planned on being married to him by then.

I got up, took my skirt and jacket off. I glanced at the clock, and realized that I didn't have that much time. Josiah would be coming home soon and Hassan usually stopped by after work. I took my drawers off and got on my knees. I pulled out his dick and started sucking, using all my head skills.

"*Aargh,*" he groaned.

I had him where I needed him. I got up and sat on his hard dick from the back. I knew I was running out of time, so I sped up the process. I felt him getting aggressive and his dick enlarging; I knew he was about to cum. I tried to jump off his dick, but he held me down with a tight grip while his cum spilled into my pussy. He finally let me go and I jumped off him while sperm rolled down my legs.

I looked at him. "Why you did that?"

"Babe, the pussy so good, I couldn't pull out. You on the pill, aren't you?"

"Hell no, I ain't on no damn pill. Damn you, Corey."

"Come on baby girl, you know I smoke a lot of weed, so my sperm count is really low."

"Boy, whatever."

"Imani, you know how I feel about you. You need to leave that nigga. All he doing is dogging you out, plus he married. Stop playing the side ho. Come fuck wit' a real nigga and I promise, I'll take care of you and my son."

"Corey, stop it! I lied to you years ago when I said I didn't love him. I love him. Better yet, I'm in love with him."

"Listen, I told you what I want; I want to be a father to my son. I gave you enough time, so either you tell him or I'ma let him know."

I walked up to him and put my arm around his neck.

"Baby, there's no need for you to tell him. I'll tell him myself, and then we can be a family. I just need a few more months to get this money, so we can start over. He's supposed to be hitting me off with over a hundred grand," I lied.

His face lit up like Christmas lights. "Oh yeah? Damn babe, you 'bout to hit the jackpot. Shit, take your time and get that paper off that fool."

"Thanks babe. I appreciate you doing this for me, for us, and for our son."

"Aiight Shorty. Lemme use the bathroom."

I watched as he walked to the bathroom. I let out a long breath.

"What the fuck is this nigga on?" I mumbled under my breath.

"Corey, I don't mean to rush you, but I got some things to do before Josiah gets home."

"Okay, okay, no sweat. Just hit me up when you're free and keep that pussy tight fo' me."

"I got you," I smiled at him.

Soon as he walked out the door, I made sure I locked it and leaned against it. *God, what am I going to do?* I thought. *You a boss bitch, don't panic*, a voice in my head answered. I made sure the door was locked again, picked my clothes up off the floor and put them in the dirty bin. Then I stormed off to the shower—had to wash this nigga's cum out of my pussy. God, why couldn't he just stay away? There was no way I could tell Hassan that Josiah was not his son. That would mess up everything. I meant everything! Tears started flowing down my face. There was no way I was going back to being broke. I knew if Hassan found out I wouldn't get the house and he would cut me and my son off.

Hassan Clarke

I was beyond pissed. How could I have been so freaking stupid as to leave the receipt for Destiny to find? And as always, she showed up and showed her ass in front of my clients. That bitch made the worst mistake of her life. It was one thing to confront me, but when she started fucking with my money, it was a new ball game.

I decided to call it a day after a few hours. I was too upset to handle any kind of business. Going home was out of the question, because I might've beat that bitch up if she came at me with any more drama. I decided to drop by to see Imani and my son. She left work in a rush today; I knew it had something to do with Destiny showing her ass earlier. I had so much on my mind. My mind was racing and I wanted it all to end. I planned to go see a divorce lawyer tomorrow. It was time to get this miserable-ass bitch out of my life for good.

As I pulled onto Imani's street and close to her address, I saw her car pull in, and another car pulled up beside her. I watched as she got out and a dude in the other car also exited his vehicle. They walked together, she opened the door, and they went inside.

I tried to call her phone, but I got no response. I wondered who the fuck that nigga was? I wanted to knock on her door, but the lawyer in me told me not to. I waited for about twenty minutes before the nigga came out the house. As he walked toward his car, I noticed his face looked familiar. When he got close enough, I realized I did know him; it was my right-hand man Corey. I was really thrown off. . . What was Corey doing coming out of Imani's house? If I recalled correctly, he never liked her. As a matter of fact, he used to tell me how she was a freak and she couldn't keep her legs closed. I sat there wondering when they had become friends.

I was tempted to jump out and beat his ass, but that nigga might've been strapped. Instead, I waited for him to pull off, then I walked to the door and rang the doorbell.

"Hey babe," she looked surprised.

"Hey yourself. Listen, this is strange: I could have sworn I seen my old partner pulling out of the parking space."

"Really? That is strange," she said.

"Bitch, why you lying?" I slapped her in the face.

"What the hell you just hit me for?" She lunged toward me.

I pushed her down on the sofa.

"I'ma ask again. What was Corey doing up in here?"

"Baby, I don't know what you talking about. I swear," she cried.

I knew that bitch was standing in front of me lying; she must've thought I was a fool.

I walked up to her, grabbed her by the throat and applied pressure.

"Get off my moms," Josiah's voice echoed.

I was so caught up in the moment I hadn't even heard when he entered the house. I looked at him and noticed he had his fist balled up. I then looked back at his mother. It was a no way out situation for me, so I let go and pushed her away from me.

"You want me to call 911 for you?"

"No baby, just go to your room."

I looked at that bitch lying on the sofa holding her face. I walked up to her and looked her dead in the eyes.

"You fucking dead to me. All the shit I did for you and you had that fuck nigga up in here. Bitch, fuck you." I spit dead on that bitch.

"Baby, I swear, I don't know where he was coming from. I swear on my dead mama's grave. . . ."I walked out before her ass finished her sentence. I hurriedly walked to my car because I wasn't sure that bitch wouldn't call the police.

I hit my steering wheel as I backed out of the parking space and raced down the street. There was nowhere for me to go, since I didn't plan on going to the house.

I decided to stop at the liquor store at 241st Street and Wakefield Avenue and grab me a bottle of Crown Royal. I needed something strong to drown out this pain I was feeling inside.

My mind traveled back years ago. There had been a rumor going around that Imani and Corey fucked around, but I didn't pay that shit no mind. I wondered how long they'd been fucking around. That nigga and that bitch were lucky that I left the streets alone. Back in the day,

I would've murked that nigga for violating me, but now I got too much money and a life ahead of me to fuck up over one piece of pussy. I wasn't goin' lie though; that bitch had my mind all the way fucked up.

I paid for a room at the Days Inn on Baychester Avenue. I took the bottle to the head; I was fuming with anger and rage. No other bitch had ever tried me like this and the one bitch that I loved was a fucking whore.

CHAPTER SEVENTEEN

Destiny Clarke

I've learned early on not to trust men. After getting raped as a child, I knew men were monsters and they could not be trusted. Finally, I found this one dude that I thought would do right by me, because I stood by him through thick and thin, good or bad. I soaked it up and played my position. I was the one that helped this bum make something of himself and this was how he repaid me. I shook my head. I was disgusted.

I was on my way to see the private investigator. He called last night asking me to meet him at his office this morning. I stayed up all night; my mind was racing. I wanted to know what Hassan had been up to, but at the same time I wasn't ready to face the music. I rang the doorbell and he buzzed me in.

"Good morning Mrs. Clarke. You look beautiful as usual."

"Thank you."

I sat across from him and the anticipation was definitely killing me.

"Okay, I'm not going to keep you waiting, but I must tell you that some of the things I'm about to share with you are deep. Your husband has been a very busy man."

"Like I told you before, I'm grown. I can handle whatever it is that you found out," I said in a serious tone.

I sat quietly as he read a list of things he found out. The main thing that grabbed my attention was when he mentioned Hassan had a fourteen-year-old son. The same fucking age as Amaiya. I sat in my seat frozen as the tears started to flow.

"Mrs. Clarke, are you okay? I can stop if you want me to."

I took a few minutes to get my emotions under control and then I spoke: "No, I'm fine. Please continue, sir."

He placed a stack of pictures in front of me. I paused. I was scared of what I was about to see. I swallowed hard and reached over to grab the pictures. In front of me was my husband. . . With his secretary? Yes, the fucking office bitch that I had a bad feeling about. The other pictures were of him and that little bitch he brought to the house. There were pictures of him and random women. All these pictures were taken within a two-week time frame. More tears fell as I sat there staring at the pictures.

"Mr. Spencer, how much do I owe you? And please put all the evidence in one envelope for me; I have to find a divorce lawyer ASAP."

"Sure, I understand. My fee is thirty-five hundred dollars and I have a colleague who is a great divorce lawyer. Trust me: call him and he'll take good care of you. Please do me one favor, though."

"And what is that?" I asked, as I wrote the check.

"Don't do anything stupid. Let the courts handle it."

I smiled at him, handed him the check, and grabbed the envelope. "Thank you, Mr. Spencer." I put my glasses on and walked out of his office.

I sat in my car with my head resting on my steering wheel. I felt like someone had taken something sharp and stabbed into my chest. I screamed out as the pain became unbearable. "Lord, give me the strength. I know

I've done some things in my life, but God, I didn't deserve this," I whispered.

After sitting there feeling sorry for myself, I regained a little bit of courage. I started the car and drove off.

I didn't feel like cooking so I ordered pizza and hot wings for Amaiya. I didn't have an appetite, so I made me a cup of herbal tea and called it a night, even though it was only seven p.m.

Now that I had all the information I needed, it was time for me to do something about it. I would call the lawyer tomorrow. It was time to get this bum ass nigga out of my life, once and for all.

Imani Gibson

I done gotten my ass into some shit I had no idea how to get out of. I didn't know Hassan would show up so early. He surprised me when he asked about Corey. My ass had to think fast. There was no way I was going to confess to him, hell no. I was taking that shit to my grave.

That nigga crossed the line when he put his hands on me. This was the man that I loved. How could he do me like that? And to disrespect me by spitting in my face? That shit hurt my soul.

After he left, my son ran to me. "Ma, you all right? I don't know why you even deal with him," he said to me with an attitude.

"I'm fine and don't talk like that. He is your father."

"Father? Ma, all he do is drop off money. He 'ont spend no time with me."

"Josiah, shut your mouth. He your daddy and he loves you. Don't you talk like that."

"Aiight Ma," he said, before he stormed off to his room.

I got up off the couch and went to the bathroom to wash the spit off my face. I looked in the mirror and that's when I busted out crying. *How he could treat me like this, after all I've been through with him?* I thought. I slowly knelt down by the tub, crying my heart out. The intensity of the pain ripped through my broken soul.

I cried until the tears stop flowing; I was all cried out. I got up and stumbled to my room, too distraught to take off my clothes, so I just lay across the bed. My mind wandered around. I twisted and turned, too restless to close my eyes. I got up, went to the kitchen, poured me a glass of wine, and drank it in one big gulp, and then I walked back into my room.

"Damn you, Hassan," I screamed out. I lay there sobbing until I dozed off.

I was up bright and early the next morning. I was still hurting from the incident last night, but I was in a different frame of mind. I got up and made breakfast for Josiah before he left for school. My apartment looked a hot mess, so I decided to clean up. Ever since I was a little girl, whenever I got upset I would start cleaning. I turned on the stereo, put in Melanie Fiona's CD, and pressed repeat. "Oh yeah. I've got trouble with my friends, trouble in my life. Problems when you don't come home at night, but when you do you always start a fight." I sang the song over and over. Something about the words gave me a bit of a boost. I dried my eyes and smiled. "Hassan, you're going to regret fucking me over," I uttered to myself.

***

I hadn't been feeling well lately. I thought it was food poisoning until I went to the emergency room. After taking a pregnancy test, the doctor told me I was pregnant.

"Are you sure?" I asked.

"Yes ma'am. Congratulations."

I sat there with my head hung low. Now it made sense; the headaches and the nausea were because I was knocked up.

"Are you okay?" the doctor asked.

"Yes. Just a little surprised is all." I smiled at her.

Soon as she left the room, I put on my clothes in a rush and left behind her. I didn't wait to sign my release paper or anything; shit they already had my insurance information.

I was not only surprised, but also devastated. Soon as the bitch mentioned pregnant, my mind rushed back to two weeks ago when I had sex with Corey and he bust inside of me. Not again God, I thought. Things were already bad enough, and now this bullshit. I tried to recall the last time I had sex with Hassan, and I believed it was the day before Corey and I fucked. A broad smile came over my face as a thought popped in my head. "Gotcha," I said as I drove down White Plains Road.

Soon as I got home, I dialed Hassan's number. He had it turned off because it kept on going to voicemail and I kept pressing redial. My happiness quickly turned to anger. He barely turned his phone off, so I knew he was on some bullshit. What if something was wrong with me and his child? Since he didn't pick up, I dialed his bitch's number. Yes, I had the new number. After Charmaine told me she changed her number, I searched Hassan's phone and got the new number. Each time she picked up, I just held the phone and breathed hard. The last time she picked up, the bitch got bold. "Listen to me little bitch, whoever you are: stop calling my fucking phone. If you're looking for Hassan, call his fucking phone," the bitch yelled in my ear and then hung up.

I was heated as hell because I didn't get any words in, so I dialed her number again, but she didn't pick up. I decided to shoot her a text:

Bitch please, just because you're married to him on paper doesn't mean you own him. He is mine, believe that.:

Who the hell is this? She texted back.

Your worst fucking nightmare bitch. He don't love you, he's only there because you got the money.

Ha-ha, you must be the whore that he's been fucking. I know who the fuck you are, you that piece of shit, so-called secretary. Listen to me, you earth disturbing bitch, you can never be me; just because he is fucking you, don't think you're special. Trust me; his cock is community property. Now leave me the hell alone before I get your ass for harassment.

I was so mad my blood pressure rose. She had no idea that I would trample her ass. I guess I'd have to her show her ass how Bronx bitches got down.

These hoes always screamed that they were the wives, but what they didn't understand was just because you were married to him on paper, didn't mean you owned him. Hassan was my man and I swear this bitch would find out soon enough.

Soon as Josiah got into the bed, I jumped up and got dressed in an all-black velour suit. I tied my hair up with my black scarf and then grabbed the biggest knife in the kitchen and the small hammer that I kept under the sink. I pulled up at their residence and looked around. There was no one outside, so I parked at the side and snuck up the driveway. His car was the first one I tackled, shattering his window and slashing his tires. I then made my move to that bitch's car. Each time I broke her window, I imagined breaking that ho's neck. All it took was about five minutes to wreak havoc on the motherfuckers who had caused me pain. After I was finished, I ran down the driveway, jumped into my car, and sped off. I laughed my ass off as I drove down the street. I wish I could've been present when they realized their shit was fucked up.

CHAPTER EIGHTEEN

Destiny Clarke

After I spoke to the lawyer that Mr. Spencer gave me, I felt much better. I gave him all the evidence that I had on Hassan. The lawyer told me we needed to find out everything about him and his finances, so he suggested hiring a forensic accountant to dig deep into Hassan's finances. That was great because whatever money he was hiding would be found.

When I got home from the lawyer's office, I noticed Hassan's car was parked in the driveway.

"What are you doing in my house?"

"I live here, you know that right?" he asked.

"I don't give a damn about that anymore. I want you out," I yelled.

"Like I said, I'm not going anywhere. You're my fucking wife, so act like you know it."

"Ha-ha, you're a cheater and a liar. I wonder what I saw in you." I spat.

He stepped aggressively toward me, and I took two steps back.

"You know what, Hassan? That bitch should have killed your ass when she was pregnant with you," I snapped.

"Watch your mouth, B." He continued coming closer to me.

I backed into the kitchen and took a quick glance of my surroundings.

"Like I told you, I'm done with you. I want you out of my life for good."

"Bitch and I told your ass, I ain't going nowhere. You heard me clearly," he yelled and lunged toward me.

I backed into the cupboard and grabbed my butcher knife.

"You better back the hell up, before I slice you into pieces."

"Bitch, fuck you. I don't care nothing about that."

"Try me, you bum. Try me!" I pointed the knife at him.

He stood there looking like a savage animal, trying to attack his prey. He must have noticed that I wasn't backing down so he looked at me and smiled.

"Bitch, I got you." He turned and walked away.

I waited five minutes and when I felt the coast was clear, I ran upstairs to my bedroom and locked my door. There was no way I was going to be in the same room as that man.

Last night was a fucking nightmare. After that altercation with Hassan, I thought I could get a little rest, but it didn't happen. Hassan's ho called my phone. Clearly, this bitch had nothing better to do than play on my damn phone. I didn't have time for this stupid ho; I was too old to be playing phone games. The next time that bitch called or texted me, I was prepared to call the police and press charges on her.

I got up and went outside to warm up the car, and got the shock of my life. All my car windows, along with Hassan's car windows were busted out and our tires were slashed.

"Fuck," I yelled as I walked back into the house.

"What's wrong?" Amaiya asked.

"Some dumb ass done slashed my tires and bust my windows out."

"What?" she said and ran outside.

I grabbed my phone and dialed the police, and then I walked upstairs to the guest room where Hassan has been sleeping. I tried to open the door, but he had it locked from the inside. I banged on the door, but he didn't say anything.

"Open the goddamn door." I banged harder.

"Man, what is it?" he opened the door.

"The police are on their way 'cause one of your whores done slashed my tires and busted out my windows."

"Whatever! I keep telling you, I ain't got no ho," he said and he slammed the door in my face.

"Don't close no door up in here. I ain't goin' keep reminding you that I want your ass gone."

I stormed downstairs when I heard a loud knock on the door. I knew it was the police department.

"Good morning ma'am. My name is Officer Darren. You called about vandalism to your property?"

"Yes, good morning. It's right out here." I stepped out the door and pointed to my car.

"Is this also your car?"

"No, that's my soon to be ex-husband's car."

The younger officer looked at me and quickly turned his head.

"Is he here?"

"Yes, he's upstairs."

I walked to the door and yelled to Amaiya, "Tell your daddy the police officers want to speak with him."

"Mrs. Clarke, do you have any idea who might have done this to your property?"

"Not at all, but there's this one lady who has been playing on my phone."

"You think she did it? Do you have her name?"

"Yes, her name is Imani Gibson. She's my husband's whore."

He shot me a strange look and continued writing in his notepad.

"Well, maybe your husband can shed some light on the situation."

He walked out the door, looking like he didn't have a care in the world.

"Hello, I'm Officer Darren and this is my partner Officer Stone. Your wife called us out here after she noticed the damage to the vehicles. Do you know of anyone that would want to damage your property?"

"Well, I'm defense attorney Hassan Clarke, so I'm pretty sure I got some enemies out there."

"Are you *the* defense attorney Hassan Clarke?"

"The one and only," this fool said, like he was proud.

"Damn my man, some of the officers down at the precinct hate when you're the defense attorney."

"Yeah I figure so, but you know I have to give my clients the best of me."

I cleared my throat. "Officer Darren, you're here to take a report of the damages on my vehicle."

Hassan shot me a dirty look, mad that I interrupted his praise party.

"Yes ma'am. Let me get the exact time you last saw your vehicle, and what time this morning you first noticed the damages. I will make the report."

I gave them everything I could. They took the report and left. Hassan walked off into the house and I followed closely on his heels.

"I know it's one of them low-class bitches that you're fucking with who fucked my shit up. It might be that office ho that called my phone last night."

"Woman, I don't have no ho or no bitches. You're delusional. It's all in your head. Keep behaving like that and I'll have your ass committed."

"Fuck you, you're the delusional one. You walk around here like your shit don't stink, but you know what? You're going to pay for it all!" I yelled.

"Mommy, why are you yelling?"

"Sorry baby. Get your stuff ready. I'm going to call a cab to take you to school."

"While you do that, get you some medicine woman," he said.

I was going to answer him, but I saw the look on my daughter's face. I stopped, and turned the other way to retrieve my cell phone. Fifteen minutes later, the taxi came and Amaiya left for school. I was happy she was gone. I hate that I had to go through this shit and she had to witness it. I swear I've always said that when I have a child, I wouldn't put her through any drama.

I was so caught up in my thoughts that I didn't see when he walked up on me.

"Bitch, what was all that shit you was talking earlier?" he grabbed my neck.

"Let me go," I tried to mumble.

I tried to grab his face, but he had me pinned against the wall.

"You unstable bitch, you going to stop disrespecting me. You hear me?" he yelled as he squeezed tighter.

I couldn't breathe and everything around me started to spin. Little stars started dancing across my blurred vision. Silent tears flowed down my face as I whispered a silent prayer, "God please protect my baby girl." I really thought my life was coming to an end.

***

"Mom, wake up! Mom, wake up!" I heard someone yelling.

I opened my eyes and saw it was my daughter.

"Mommy, are you okay? Why were you on the ground?"

"Baby, I must have fell out. I wasn't feeling too good."

"Come on, get up." She tried to pull me up.

I stumbled to my feet, I was feeling out of it, but with Amaiya's help, I managed to get to the couch.

"Here's some orange juice. Drink it," she demanded.

My throat felt dry, so I welcomed the juice. I felt a lump in my throat as I swallowed. I rubbed my hands across my neck and it felt sore and it was hurting badly.

"Grab me a warm washcloth."

"You sure you all right? You want me to call Daddy?"

"No, no, no, don't call your daddy. I'm fine. I just need to go lie down."

I used the warm washcloth to apply heat to my neck. I walked to the bathroom and cut on the bright light, raising my head so I could take a look at my neck—red marks were visible. I rubbed my hands across the spot; it felt raw. Something inside of me was heating up. My temper was rising. Tears welled up in my eyes. I was abused as a child and now I felt violated, again. I vowed years ago that I wouldn't let another man abuse me, whether it was sexually, mentally, or physically.

I stared at myself in the mirror. I didn't recognize the woman I'd become. A weak, fragile woman was staring back at me. *How did I get here?* I wondered. Pity turned into anger. My heart was broken, but I still loved him. My mind kept tugging at me, letting me know that I deserved better. I couldn't stand the sight of my reflection in the mirror, so I cut off the light and walked out of the bathroom, got into my bed, and cried my heart out. I felt so broken, like there was no hope, none whatsoever.

Hassan Clarke

After staying at the hotel for a few days, I decided to go home. Being a lawyer, I knew the law and I knew Destiny could not put me out. Funny thing was her dumb ass thought I would just up and leave. Don't get me wrong: I wanted to leave. Nah, correct that, I was *going* to leave, but I wanted to wait until she calmed down, so I could talk to her. I knew if we let the divorce play out in the courts, she was going to get half of my money and truthfully, I didn't plan on giving her a dime. This was my hard-earned money and the only thing I was prepared to give her was child support, even though I was not sure Amaiya was my child. Mama and the rest of my family have been screaming for me to get a DNA test ever since she was born, but my ass was too hardheaded to listen.

For days, I walked around on pins and needles. I hoped Imani didn't call the cops. There was no way I was going to the slammer. I laughed to myself, the thought of me going to jail made me chuckle. I wasn't a punk and I'd never been to jail and didn't plan on going any time in the future.

Ever since I started making money, it seemed as if trouble had a way of following me. I had enough problems to deal with, and one of these stupid bitches made it worse by coming to the crib and fucking my shit up. I knew it wasn't Tanya, 'cause she 'ont be on that bullshit. Everything in my gut was screaming that this was Imani's doing. She wouldn't stop calling me; it got so bad I had to cut off my phone. I just wasn't in the mood to talk to her. I had to play it off though, because there was no way I was going to tell Destiny the secretary fucked her shit up.

Racquel Williams

After the police left, I was about to get dressed and head to work. Destiny's annoying ass felt the need to continue talking down on me. I had to let that bitch know that I didn't have a problem with hitting a ho upside the head. These hoes kept playing and woke the beast inside of me. I was seconds away from ending that bitch's life. I snapped and squeezed as tight as my hands allowed me to. I had no intention to let up until that ho was dead. The only reason she was breathing was because my phone started ringing repeatedly. I let her go and stormed out of the house.

CHAPTER NINETEEN

Destiny Clarke

This was the first time I had a good night's sleep in a while. I went to bed around nine p.m. and didn't get up until around ten a.m. I had a doctor's appointment. For the past week or so, I'd had a burning sensation when I peed and severe itching. I thought it was the soap I used since I recently switched from Oil of Olay body wash to Dove body wash. Everything changed yesterday when the burning got so bad, I was scared to pee and when I did, it was unbearable.

I anxiously sat in the waiting room. I felt nervous and agitated. I'd never had a STD in my entire life, but here I was at thirty-eight years old, talking about my burning. At first, I felt embarrassed, but being a nurse I knew that I had to get checked out. In my heart, I was hoping that I was wrong.

"Mrs. Clarke," the nurse called my name.

"Here."

"Follow me please."

She took my vitals and asked a few personal questions.

"So what brought you here today?" she asked.

I paused for a little, and then took a deep breath. "Whenever I pee, it burns. Also, I have a smelly discharge and I'm itchy."

"How long have you had these symptoms?"

"The burning sensation has been going on for about a week and the discharge started a few days ago."

"Okay, follow me, we're going to room B."

"Here's a gown, take off everything on the bottom. Here's a cup for your urine. The bathroom is the first door to the left. Dr. Li Yung will be in shortly."

Dr. Li Yung finally showed up after I waited for over forty-five minutes.

"Mrs. Clarke, nice to see you again."

I explained everything that has been going on with me for the past week. He decided to do a pelvic exam, collected some specimen and sent them off to the lab.

The anticipation was killing me. I tried to stay positive, hoping for the best. It was a little over two hours when he walked back into the room with my chart."Mrs. Clarke, your results are back from the lab, and it is confirmed that you have contracted gonorrhea and trichomoniasis. The test for herpes will be back in a few days. You might want to inform your sexual partner so he can get tested too. I'm going to give you a shot of Ceftriaxone to treat the gonorrhea and also an oral dose of Azithromycin. As for the trichomoniasis, I'm going to prescribe Flagyl. Please take all the pills until they are finished. Also, please refrain from having any sexual intercourse until all symptoms are gone."

I sat there, looking dumbfounded. Did this doctor just tell me that my pussy was burning because this dirty cock man gave me some shit? I sat there with my fist balled up. I used every bit of strength inside of me to prevent the tears from flowing. I stopped listening to the doctor. Nothing he was saying could help what I was feeling. Soon as he walked out the room, I felt a tear drop fall on my arm. I quickly wiped it away. *I don't need to cry*, I kept telling myself.

The doctor and the nurse returned shortly. He gave me a shot in my butt, which hurt like hell, but I didn't flinch.

The physical pain was no comparison to the mental anguish I was experiencing. The nurse handed me a pill with a cup of water.

"Okay, Mrs. Clarke, you're all set. I'm going to write the prescription for the antibiotics. I want you to come back in here in a week for a follow up. I will also let you know when your other test is back. Take care." He smiled.

"Thank you, Dr. Li Yung."

I got off the bed and got dressed. I was anxious to get out of the office. Minutes later, the nurse returned with a prescription slip and my discharge papers. I quickly signed the paper, took the slip and walked out in a hurry.

I dug into my purse and found my car keys. I was shaking so badly, it took me a few tries before I got the keys into the hole. I got into my car, slammed the door, and placed my head on my steering wheel. That's when the tears started to flow. I knew better, I was a nurse, but I trusted my husband and this was what he did to me. A sharp pain ripped across the left side of my chest. I grabbed my chest. I hoped it wasn't a heart attack. Being a nurse, I knew that I wasn't too young to have one of those. I began to feel lightheaded and the pain shifted to the middle of my chest. My breathing wasn't normal and I gasped for air, but I could barely breathe. I tried reaching for my purse to get my phone so I could dial 911. I couldn't reach it. Instead, my head hit the steering wheel. The horn started going off.

Imani Gibson

After not communicating with me for weeks, Hassan had the nerve to call my phone, asking if I was the one that busted out his window and slashed his tires.

"Boy, no. I have no idea what you talking about," I blatantly lied.

"I swear on my mom's, B, if I find out you did that fuck shit, I'm going to beat your ass for real."

"Hassan, whatever you say. Ain't nobody scared of your ass and like I told you, it wasn't me. It might be one of them hoes you fucking."

"Imani, grow the fuck up," he yelled.

"I'll grow up soon as you grow some balls like a man and stop slinging your dick everywhere," I spat.

"Man, whatever. I'll be over there later to check on my little man."

"I'm not going to be home."

"Your ass better be home. I ain't seen my little man in a while,'cause your dumb ass still want to be a ho and shit."

"Boy, fuck you. I ain't no ho and if I was fucking another nigga, trust me, I have all rights because you're a married man." I hung up the phone before he could get a response in.

I didn't get a chance to put the phone down before it started ringing again.

"Hassan, what the hell you want?" I mumbled.

I looked at the caller ID and noticed it wasn't him. It was his sister Charmaine.

Oh man, I'm really not in the mood, I thought.

"Hello," I said.

"Damn bitch, why you sound like you lost your best friend? I ain't dead."

"Nah, just tired. That's all."

"Well, take your ass to sleep. I guess you too tired to hear what I gotta tell you."

"Why you playing? You know I'm never too tired to hear some juicy gossip."

"My brother's wife is in the hospital. The bitch had a heart attack."

"Bitch, you lying." I sat up on the bed.

"Nah, Hassan called Mama. She is in South Shore Hospital."

"I wonder what brought on that heart attack."

"Girl, I 'ont know, but Mama said that bitch almost died."

"I wonder how your brother feels about that. He might be hurting," I said sarcastically.

"Like you really give a fuck about that bitch," Charmaine burst out laughing.

"I know you goin' at least let me pretend like I give two fucks. It might not be a bad idea for that bitch to croak so Hassan and I can live happily ever after and before you say anything negative, I love him, and I plan on being his woman."

"I ain't saying shit. If you like it, then I love it. Anyway I gotta run, talk to you later."

"Aiight, later."

I lay back down, digesting the latest news. I wished that bitch was dead for real. I swear, I wanted to confront her ass, so I could let her know he don't love her.

Hassan Clarke

My day at work started all wrong. I learned that the jury came back with a guilty verdict on one of the biggest cases that my firm handled. I put on a very strong argument in the closing statement and I thought it would've went our way. I guess better luck next time. I hated losing, whether it was business or personal.

I had so much anger built up inside of me that I could kill Destiny with my bare hands. When I was broke and out I had no choice but to kiss her ass. Those days are long gone; now I made well over six figures a year. What could I possibly need her for? That bitch kept trying to put me out, but I wasn't going anywhere until I got all my finances situated. I couldn't hide a lump sum all at once because I didn't want the government in my business. I wanted to make sure there would be no trace of any kind of money when and if we ended up in divorce court.

After weeks of not dealing with Imani, I finally decided to hit her up. I wasn't goin' front: every time I thought about Corey fucking her, I got pissed and I couldn't shake the feeling. Even though she kept denying it, I wasn't a fool and deep in my guts, I knew he was smashing my bitch. I couldn't take it anymore, so I decided to go around the way to check Corey. I wanted to see what he got to say about Imani. It'd been two years since I'd been to Edenwald Projects, but it was where I was born and raised. A few niggas I grew up with still lived over there. I had no other way to reach this nigga, so I decided to stop at Ms. Dorothy's house. She was Corey's grandmother; she raised him and his sisters' right after his father killed their mother and then himself.

As I parked my car and walked toward the buildings, I took a quick glance at my surroundings. Even though I grew up around here and was considered one of them, I didn't trust these niggas; these dudes be hating hard, especially if you was one of them and you moved out and made a better life.

I knocked on Ms. Dorothy's door, but no one answered. I banged a few more times, and there still was no answer.

An elderly woman from the next-door apartment peeped out and said, "Keep that noise down."

"I apologize, but I was looking for Ms. Dorothy."

"Who are you? You look familiar. Do I know you?" she asked.

"I'm not sure. I grew up three doors down. Ms.Paulette is my mother."

"Paulette. . . Paulette, I remember her. She moved a few years back. Well, you must not have heard. Dorothy passed away about a year or so ago. She had cancer. She was such a good soul."

"No, I didn't hear that." I turned to walk away.

"Wait, what's your name?" she asked.

"Hassan."

"All right Hassim, you take care and tell your mother I send my regards."

"I sure will." I shook my head and walked off, I had no idea why older people always messed someone's name up.

It was sad to hear of Ms. Dorothy's passing. That lady played an important role in my life when I was growing up.

On my way back to my car, I passed by a few old heads playing dominoes. I nodded my head to acknowledge them. I saw much hadn't changed around the way; everything looked the same.

My phone started ringing; I looked at the caller ID and noticed it was Amaiya.

"Hey baby girl."

"Daddy, Mommy is in the hospital. She had a heart attack," she yelled.

"Say what, baby? Calm down. I'm trying to understand you."

"I said Mama had a heart attack and she's at South Shore Hospital."

"What? Who told you that? I ain't get no phone call."

"Grandma came and picked me up from school. We're on our way to the hospital."

"Damn. Calm down, baby. I have to go to the office first and then I'll be there shortly."

"Did you hear me? I said Mom is in the hospital and you're talking about you got to go to the office," she raised her voice.

"Watch your mouth. I said I'll be there." All I heard was the dial tone in my ear.

Her ass needed to be grounded. She knew damn well that I 'ont play that disrespectful shit. I didn't mean to sound cold or anything like that, but if this was a phone call telling me that bitch was dead, I would've felt much better. I would not have had to worry about no divorce and giving her any of my money.

I went back to the office to handle some business. Two new clients came in who needed me on their drug cases ASAP. Just because she was up in a hospital didn't mean I had to stop my money flow.

I finally locked up the office about a quarter after six. I got on the expressway and headed to New Rochelle. When I got there, I walked into the lobby. Before I was able to talk to the receptionist to let her know why was there, I spotted my mother-in-law. She wasn't too fond of me, and I didn't like the old bitch. If you asked me, I honestly thought the old bitch was jealous and just wanted some of this good dick. I headed over to where they were seated.

"Ms. Jackson."

"Hmm. . . My daughter is laying up in here fighting for her life and your worthless behind just now rolling up in here." She shook her head in disgust.

"Grandma, you promised not to start nothing," Amaiya said.

"Sorry, grandbaby."

"Baby girl, what are they saying about yo' mama's condition?" I asked.

"Amaiya, go get some snacks. You been here for a while." she handed her a twenty-dollar bill.

"You know, I have no idea what my daughter sees in you. I see you for the piece of shit you are. You can dress up in that fancy suit, but underneath all that you're nothing but a two-headed snake. You're the reason why my daughter is in the hospital. I will be happy when she gets rid of your sorry behind."

"Lady, you should be ashamed of yourself, talking like that. However, I do see where your daughter got her bitterness from." Amaiya returned before I could finish telling this old bitch how I really felt.

I walked away to find the doctor and was told he'd be out in a few minutes. I walked to the other side of the waiting room; I didn't want to be near that old bitch and her ranting. Twenty minutes later, the doctor emerged from this area. I got up and walked over to him.

"I understand your wife is Destiny Clarke. The ambulance brought her into the emergency room today. She suffered a minor heart attack. Sometimes when patients are subject to a minor heart attack, it's assumed that it's not serious, but the facts are that even a mild heart attack can result in heart damage and can also cause permanent damage. A second heart attack is also imminent."

"So what are her chances of fully recovering?"

"That I can't tell you right now. We will continue monitoring her situation. We are providing her with the best care she could possibly get."

"Okay. When can I see her?"

"Actually, she's sedated and needs to rest, but you can go in for a few minutes."

"Thanks, Doc," I said as I followed him to Destiny's room.

Soon as I walked in, I noticed that she was hooked up to different wires and machines were everywhere. Her eyes were closed, so I walked closer to her so I could get a better look. She looked so helpless, so different from the bitch that couldn't shut her mouth for a second.

I stood over her, looking at the cold bitch that I married. As a husband with a sick wife, I was supposed to be feeling all emotional and hurt, but I didn't feel anything.

"Why couldn't you just die?" I mumbled under my breath.

I glanced at the extra pillow on the bed. The thought of using it to suffocate her crossed my mind, but my thoughts were interrupted by the doctor.

"She needs to get some rest, but you are welcome to stay if you want," the doctor said.

"No, he don't need to stay. I'm staying with my daughter," this old bitch said, as she walked into the room.

"I'm sorry, Ms. Jackson, but he's the next of kin so he's allowed to stay."

"That's fine. She can stay with her daughter. I'm going to take my daughter home. It's getting late and she has school in the morning." I immediately left the room and walked over to Amaiya.

"Let's go home, baby." I grabbed her arm.

"I want to stay with my mom." She pulled her arm away from me.

"No, you can't stay with your mother. It's almost ten o'clock and you have school in the morning. Now let's go, little girl," I said. I was too annoyed.

I'd had enough bullshit for one day and was ready to get away from it all.

CHAPTER TWENTY

Destiny Clarke

I woke up in a hospital feeling kind of groggy from being heavily sedated. Soon as I opened my eyes, I saw Mama sitting down in the chair by my bed.

"Hey baby, you awake?" She squeezed my hand.

"Hey Mama. Where's Amaiya?"

"She's at school right now. She'll be up here later to see you."

"Okay, and Hassan?"

"His sorry behind will be up here later, but don't worry about all that. Focus on your health and getting better."

"I know, Mama. I consider myself pretty healthy, so I was shocked when the doctor told me that I had a mild heart attack. I tell you, age don't matter these days."

"Yes, but lately you've been under extreme stress. You don't say a lot, but I see it written all over your face. You're always sad and not your usual bubbly self."

I agreed with everything she was saying to me, but I was feeling down and wasn't in the mood to really discuss the situation between Hassan and me.

Mama held my hand and started to pray aloud. No matter what was going on, you could count on her to call on Jesus's name. I was never a religious person, but I was grateful that the man above had my back. Thinking back, I really thought I was about to die in that parking garage. I was tired and Mama had errands to run, so she left and I decided to take a nap.

***

"Hey babe," Hassan said when he walked into my room.

"Don't 'hey babe' me, you son of a bitch. I was waiting on the right time to confront you. Your nasty ass done gave me some fucking STDs!"

"What? I ain't give you shit. I know you want to get rid of me, but accusing me of some fuck shit like that is crazy."

I took a deep breath; I knew I shouldn't be getting myself all worked up. I was tired of lying in this bed and watching him come up in here, pretending like he was the doting husband.

"You know what, Hassan? I'm a grown ass woman that is married to one man, which means I'm only screwing one man. That one man is you. Like I said, your dirty cock done gave me two fucking sexually transmitted diseases."

"I hear all that you're saying and I'll say it again: I ain't give you shit. If I had an STD, I'm pretty sure I would have known."

I wanted to get far away from this two-timing pig. Just being in his presence made me sick to my stomach.

"Ha ha, you're freaking ridiculous. You better go get your cock tested and make sure that ho you fucking gets tested also. I hope you wasn't eating her pussy too, because that shit might be in your throat."

"Man chill out with all that. The only woman's pussy I ate is yours. I don't even get down like that."

This fool must've forgotten he was not in the court-house. He was talking to me, the woman that knows all his fucked up ways. I pushed the button for the nurse.

"Hello Mrs. Clarke, this is Nurse Scott, how may I help you?"

"I need to talk to you."

"Okay, I'll be in there."

I turned my head and closed my eyes. As far as I was concerned, the conversation between us was over.

"What may I help you with?" Nurse Scott asked when she entered the room.

"I want him to get out of my room and I need to put him on the no-contact list at the hospital."

"What...what are you doing?" he looked at me puzzled. "Mrs. Clarke, are you sure?"

"Yes ma'am, I'm the patient and I have that right."

"Mr. Clarke, she's right. She has the right to refuse visitors. I'm going to have to ask you to leave the room and the premises."

"Yo, B, you tripping," he said as he walked out

"Thank you, nurse, and please let the front desk know that I don't want him to visit or to call on the telephone."

"I will let them know. Now you need to get some rest. I don't know what's going on, but your health is more important. Try not to stress yourself out," she said and then walked out.

I was too tired. . . I rolled over and dozed off.

Imani Gibson

Hassan said he was on his way over here. I sure missed my daddy. I didn't care what we went through—I still loved him. His sister and other bitches thought I was stupid for being with him. A bitch like me wasn't stupid; I knew how to play my position. There was no way I was going to walk away from my man for the next ho to have him. I figured if I stuck around long enough, that ho would get tired of him cheating and she would get rid of him. Guess who would be there to pick him up? Yep that's right; his wifey.

Corey kept calling my phone, constantly asking if I told Hassan about him and I. I really regretted sleeping with him again because his behavior had been unpredictable and I was more worried because he knew where I stayed at, I was scared that fool might pop up over here.

I took a shower and while washing my pussy, I stuck my finger in my hole and smelled it. A bad odor hit me in the face, which was strange. Maybe I just needed to douche, so I reached over and grabbed the Summer's Eve; I had to make sure my pussy was on point for Hassan. Nine times out of ten, he would want sex and I would be ready to give it to him.

I heard a bang on the door and I knew it was him, so I popped the door open with a smile on my face. I was shocked to see he had an angry look on his face, so different from the pleasant conversation we had earlier. He pushed past me and I let out a long sigh. What the hell is the problem now, I thought. I locked the door and walked toward him.

"What's wrong with you? You was fine when we talked earlier."

"Sit down," he demanded.

"Why?" I was getting nervous.

"Sit the fuck down, Imani," he yelled.

I saw his temper was flaring up. Whatever got him so angry must be serious, I thought

"I'm only going to ask you this once, so please think before you answer."

"Boy, what is it?"

"Who you been fucking?"

"I ain't fucking nobody. I done told yo ass before. What's this about? Is it because I told you I'm pregnant?"

"Fuck you being pregnant. That shit ain't mine. Nah, I just came from seeing Destiny and she told me I gave her some kind of sexually transmitted disease. See, this is it: you're the only one outside of her that I'm fucking raw."

"What the fuck? So let me get this right. You told me you ain't been sleeping with her, but here you are telling me you been fucking her raw. Well, you better check that bitch, if she got anything, it must be from a nigga she's fucking, 'cause I ain't got shit."

I stood up, looking at him. Whatever I said must've angered him. He stepped closer toward me and punched me in my left eye; it instantly blurred my vision.

"*Aargh*," I screamed out and covered my eye.

My screams didn't stop him. He followed up with another punch that landed me on the floor. "Oh my God, help! Help!" I screamed.

My face was hurting and I lay helplessly on the floor.

"Shut up, bitch. I told yo' ass not to lie to me. I fucking risked everything for yo' ass and this is how you repay me, huh bitch?" he yelled.

I think God heard my cries and intervened on my behalf because there was a loud knock on the door. I was too scared to even move. I touched my face and realized it was swollen. I started screaming louder. He didn't pay me any mind. Instead, he walked over to the door.

"Ain't this a bitch? Guess who was at the door? Your boyfriend Corey."

I almost fainted when he said Corey's name. *Why Lord, Why?* I thought. Anxiety was kicking in and I wished I could just disappear.

"Get up, bitch; come let this nigga in, so he can join the party."

"I'm not doing anything. He ain't got nothing to do with u. . . ." Before I could finish my sentence, I felt his foot land in my rib cage.

"No!" I screamed out.

"Now, get the fuck up bitch." He grabbed my arm.

I limped over to the door; I was hoping Corey was gone.

"Open it," he yelled.

I opened the door and like an idiot, Corey's ass stood there smiling from ear-to-ear.

"Hey babe, I was over this side of town so I decided to stop by to see you and my lil' man."

I tried to use facial expression to let him know Hassan was here, but this dumb-ass nigga wouldn't shut up.

"Corey my man, what's good?" Hassan stepped from behind the door.

"Hassan, that's you partner?" Corey asked. By the sound of his voice, I could tell he was caught off guard.

"Yeah, this me player. Come in, I need to holler at you."

I hoped Corey would've said no. Instead, this fool stepped inside.

"What's wrong with your face? And why you crying?" he asked me.

I wanted to tell him, but I couldn't bring myself to say the words.

"Yo', answer me, who did this to you?"

"Yo' partner, I 'ont think this concerns you."

"No disrespect bro, but this my son's mother, so it do concern me."

Hassan took several steps closer toward Corey. "What the fuck did you just say to me?"

"You heard me right. Josiah is my son and she is his mother, so she is my responsibility."

Hassan turned to face me. "Yo' bitch, what the fuck this nigga saying?"

I stood still, crying. *How could this happen*, I thought.

"Mani, tell him. We've been hiding this too long. Let this nigga know who your baby daddy is," Corey said sarcastically.

I knew it was my time to talk, but I was speechless. The words wouldn't come out.

"Bitch, you better start talking before I beat your ass again." Hassan stormed toward me.

Corey pulled out a gun and pointed it at Hassan. "Back the fuck up, nigga."

Oh my God, no! The situation was deteriorating by the seconds. What was this fool doing with a gun? *Jesus please take the wheel*, I thought.

"Damn, nigga, it's like that? You goin' let a bitch come between us? We brothers. We grew up together, slept in the same bed, and ate out of the same pot." Hassan seemed surprised.

"Nah bro, fuck all that. You ain't one of us. You got that degree and said fuck us. Mani is my woman and Josiah is my motherfucking seed."

"Y'all stop it!" I shouted.

"Damn it's like this Imani? You played me like that and with my so-called right hand man? I guess I should have listened when they told me you was a ho," Hassan chuckled.

"Hassan, I'm sorry. I didn't mean for you to know about Josiah like this. I wanted to tell you, but I didn't know how." I started to cry.

"Nah babe, you ain't got to apologize to this nigga. You don't need his ass no more. I'm going to take care of you and my son."

"Shut up Corey! There is no us. I love Hassan, not you. For fifteen years, I lived with regrets of fucking you. I don't want you."

"Damn B, you regret? You acting like it was a one-time deal. Matter of fact, we fucked about two months ago.

Hassan looked at me and gave me a devilish grin. "You dirty bitch! That's who knocked you up again."

"Wait, what? You pregnant again?"

"It ain't yours. It's Hassan's baby," I spat.

"How you know that? I fucked you raw and nutted in your pussy. Remember?"

"Shut the fuck up, Corey. I ain't fuck you but once. You trying to make Hassan jealous."

"Jealous? Bitch, I'm good. He can have you. I 'ont want you, I'm done. Fuck you and your son. And nigga, you just made the worst mistake of your life," Hassan yelled, before he walked out the door.

I ran behind him, but he shut the door in my face. I fell to my knees. My life was over and my heart was ripped from my body.

"No, God! Nooooo! Hassan, I love you," I bawled out.

"Babe, cut all that crying out. You only want him, 'cause he got that money. Fuck that. I can take care of you."

I held onto the couch for balance and stood up. My eyes were swollen and I could barely see.

"What part of 'I love Hassan,' don't you understand? I loved him when he had no money. I don't want to be with you."

"Man, whatever. I ain't tryna hear that shit. I'm 'bout to bounce. Hit me up when you calm down. Stop stressing. I don't want you to lose our baby."

"Fuck you, Corey. You fucked up my life. I fucking hate you, you hear me? You better stay away from me and my son."

"Whatever, Imani. Go look at your face and see what the nigga that you loving did to you." He tucked the gun back into his waist and walked out the door.

I locked the door and broke down. Everything happened so fast I didn't have time to digest it all. I walked to the bathroom to get some pain medicine. My rib cage was still hurting, so I took two Aleve to help relieve the pain. I cut the light on so I could take a look at my face in the mirror. I didn't recognize the person staring back at me. My face was swollen and red; it seemed like a truck just ran over it. I went to the fridge to grab me some ice so I could at least try to get the swelling down. I couldn't stop the tears from flowing and I was also worried about my Josiah seeing me like this. If he did, he would ask who did this to me.

Speaking of Josiah, an hour later, I heard his keys opening the door.

"Hey baby," I barely uttered because my mouth was hurting when I opened it.

"Ma, where you at? Dad called me."

"I'm in here. I don't feel too good so I'm lying down. What your dad wanted?"

He pushed my door open; I saw tears coming down his face. I wasn't worried about myself anymore. My baby was crying and that's all that mattered.

"What's wrong, Josiah? Talk to me baby."

"Dad called me when I was on my way home, talking about he ain't my dad. Some dude named Corey is my dad. Ma, what he's talking about?"

The look on his face let me know he was hurting. "Mama what is he talking about?"

I swallowed hard and looked at my son. I realized there was no way he was going to ease up or give me an easy way out. "Answer me, Mama," he said as he stepped closer to me.

"What happened to you?" he reached out and touched my face.

"Nothing, baby. I bumped into the wall."

"Ma, did Dad do this to you?"

"Baby, no your dad didn't do it."

"So who hit you, then? I ain't no fool. I know you ain't bump into no wall."

"Josiah, please listen to your mama. Hassan is your daddy and can't nobody change that. You hear me?"

"So why he saying that? To top that off now I see your face."

"Your daddy's a bit upset about some grown stuff, but trust me, he is your daddy." I smiled at him.

I was trying my best to let him off easy. I swear I didn't want my son to know that Hassan wasn't his dad.

"I swear I'ma get me a burner 'cause don't no nigga have the right to hit you like that."

"Boy, shut up talking like that. You better not be out there messing with no gun. You hear me, Josiah?"

Without responding, he walked out of the room and slammed the door behind him. Any other time, I would have got up and served his ass for being disrespectful, but I knew he was hurting.

I had no idea why Hassan had to be so cruel. He didn't have to call Josiah. He could've allowed me to handle it. I guess he made the call to hurt me, but instead, he hurt my child. I bust out crying again. The more I thought about not having Hassan in my life, the worse it became. I grabbed the pillow and dug my head deep into it, screaming my lungs out. There was no reason for me to keep living.

Hassan Clarke

Bitches weren't worth anything these days. I should've listened to my pops when he warned me about these hoes. Chris Brown ain't lie when he said, "These hoes aint loyal." I was sitting in a hotel room basking in self-pity. That bitch Imani did the ultimate betrayal. She led me to believe for fifteen years that Josiah was my son. Now this lame-ass nigga claiming that he's the daddy. I'd never felt so low in my life before now. I was a fucking sucka, playing daddy, and spending my damn money on a motherfucker that ain't even mine.

I risked everything to be with this bitch, even fucked up my relationship with Destiny. I thought Imani was the only woman for me. I had no idea she was a whore. I knew that I was living a double life, but I was in love with her ass and I was about to leave all these hoes so she and I could settle down. Things were all the way fucked up. I took another swig of the Hennessy Black. That bitch violated me, fuck her; I was going to show her and that pussy ass nigga that I wasn't to be fucked with.

I spent the rest of the night drinking and plotting. As a lawyer, I couldn't get my hands dirty, but that didn't mean a nigga couldn't get touched.

I jumped up to the ringing of my phone. I grabbed it off the dresser and put it under my pillow to muffle the sound. Whoever it was wasn't giving up.

"Fuck," I yelled and grabbed the phone.

"Hello," I said angrily.

"Daddy, where are you? Do you know what time it is?" Amaiya yelled.

"First off, little girl, lower your damn voice. Now what's up?"

"I was supposed to be at school an hour ago; now it's after nine and you still not here to pick me up."

"Why you ain't call your grandma, or better yet, why your little ass didn't get on the bus?"

"Grandma is at the hospital with Mama and I can't get on the bus because you was supposed to give me lunch money."

"All right, all right. You ready?"

"Yes, I'm ready."

I hung up the phone and rubbed my face. This little girl didn't know when to shut up. Did she just say it was after nine? Fuck, I had to be in court at ten. I looked at the time and it read 9:07 a.m. There was no way I could have made it home, got dressed, dropped her off and then made it downtown. The traffic was bumper to bumper going into Manhattan in the mornings. I scratched my head, trying to figure out what to do about Amaiya.

I dialed Tanya's number. I knew this wasn't a good look, but fuck it, I was desperate.

"Hey babe," she answered.

"Hey love, I need a huge favor."

"What's going on?"

"I need you to pick up my daughter and drop her off at school. Also, give her twenty dollars for me until I see you later."

"Really? What your wife goin' say about that?"

"Tanya baby, no disrespect, but let me worry about Destiny."

"Okay. Where is she?"

"She's at the house. I'm about to call her and let her know you're on your way. Thanks, babe. I owe you one."

I was relieved. I wished Tanya were the kind of woman that I could settle down with. She was great for a toy, but because of her race, it was definitely out of the question for me.

I dialed Amaiya's phone to let her know Tanya was going to pick her up.

"Amaiya, I can't make it to pick you up because I have to head to work, but this lady will be there to pick you up. She's driving a silver BMW. Make sure you ready."

"Lady? Who is she and does Mom know?"

"I'm not getting into all this right now. I gotta go, but I'll see you later." I hung up before she could say another word.

Destiny Clarke

I was happy to be released from the hospital. There was something about that place I couldn't stand and, to top it off, the food was horrible. Mama had been bringing me some of her good home-cooked meals and that was the only reason I hadn't snapped on these people.

"You ready baby girl?" Mama said.

"Yes ma'am. I been ready two weeks ago," I joked.

The nurse pushed me in the wheelchair while Mama walked alongside me.

After we got into the car, Mama looked at me. "So how you really feeling?"

"I'll tell you this: I'm feeling a lot better than I did. Not feeling a hundred percent yet, though."

"I'm happy you made it. God knows my heart couldn't take it if anything happened to you."

"Well Mama, I'm still here and I'm just grateful."

"Well, I know this might be too soon, but you need to see about that divorce lawyer. Don't sit around and wait for him to stress you out again."

"Mama, you must've read my mind. For the last couple of days, that's all I've been thinking about. You know, for years I used to say I'm leaving him, but I was fooling myself. It wasn't until he burned me with some STDs, that I finally decided enough was enough. That's some shit that I can't get over."

"STDs? You ain't mention nothing about that. What the hell?"

"I didn't say anything, because I found out the same day I had the heart attack."

"That dirty bastard! Someone needs to put him out of his misery."

"Mama, you know I never loved a man after what happened to me. This time I could actually say that I loved Hassan, only to find out he wasn't worth a damn. Sometimes it still bugs me. Why didn't I see him for what he really was? Am I that gullible and gone over this man that I couldn't see through the foolery?"

"Baby girl, don't blame yourself. Snakes come in all forms and sizes. You had no reason to doubt him until he showed you his real colors. If you ask me, you should've got rid of his sorry behind a long time ago. You and Amaiya deserve so much more."

I wanted to cry, because her words were reaching my soul. However, I didn't want to be weak. From now on, I refused to be weak because of this man.

***

Mama dropped me off at home and I was grateful to be back in my own space. The minute I opened the door, I noticed the place looked like a tornado had passed through. I was tempted to grab my cleaning supplies and start scrubbing, but I decided against it. This was my first day home and the only thing I wanted to do was lay in my own bed. I took a well-needed bath to help relax my mind a little; I had some serious decisions to make and I had to be prepared. After thirty minutes, I got out of the bath and my body felt much better. I got dressed, made me a bowl of soup, and got in bed.

"Mama, Mama," Amaiya ran up the stairs yelling.

"Quit all that yelling child," I said.

She didn't respond. Instead, she jumped on me, hugging and kissing me.

"Girl stop! Get off me with your school clothes. I told you there are a lot of germs running around in that school."

"Mama, you got OCD. Grandma told me you was at home and I couldn't wait to see you. I missed you so much, Mama."

"I missed you too, baby girl. How you been doing?"

"I'm good. I just missed you and Daddy don't never be around. I don't know what's going on with him lately. He seems so different."

"Baby." I took her hand into mine. I paused for a second. I didn't know how to tell my baby girl that her mommy and daddy weren't going to be together. I held her hands tight.

"What is Ma? You're scaring me."

"Baby girl, I wanted to be the first one to tell you. I'm going to divorce your daddy."

"Is it because of that lady?" she asked.

"What lady?" I blurted out.

"Oh, the lady that picked me up this morning and took me to school." I sat up in the bed. My mood went from joyous to bitter.

"What do you mean she picked you up? Where was your damn father?"

"Ma, calm down. Daddy was late coming to pick me up this morning so I called him. He said he had to be in court and someone was coming to pick me up."

"What the hell she look like?"

"Young white woman."

"That bastard!" I yelled.

"Mama, calm down. All that yelling is not good for you. Grandma told me you got to take it easy."

I knew she was right and I felt foolish. She was only fifteen, yet she was acting like the grown up and I was behaving like the child. I started to cry; every time I thought I was a step ahead, this bastard did some more fucked up shit to drag me back down. Amaiya scooted closer and laid my head on her shoulder.

"Mama, I know I'm still a child, but I'm not a baby anymore. I see how he treats you. He calls you all kinds of names. I always wished you would leave him. You're not happy like you used to be and I'm tired of seeing you hurt."

I hollered louder as I heard the words that were spoken by my child. Just the other day she was a baby and here she was, telling me some real shit. I put my arms around her and held her tight.

"You know what, Amaiya? I love you with everything in me. You hear me little girl?"

"Ma, stop, you squeezing me too tight."

"Sorry babe, I got carried away a little. Now take off your school clothes and you can call to order pizza and wings."

"Okay Mom. Love you, now get some rest." I watched as she stepped out of my room singing some rap song under her breath. "Lord help me, this child is no longer a baby," I said.

I couldn't sleep last night after what Amaiya told me. I was more determined to get this bum out of my life for good. It wasn't enough for him to cheat; he also had to have his ho around my child.I made a cup of ginger tea and then called the attorney. I hadn't spoken with him since I was admitted to the hospital. I made an appointment to go into the office the next day. I didn't want to wait another damn minute.

Mama called almost every hour since I came home. It was a great feeling to have someone who cared, but I just needed a break to myself. These last few months had been crazy and I had a gut feeling it was going to get worse. I was thinking about selling this place after the divorce. I didn't want to be reminded of him in no way. *I swear I'm done*, I kept reminding myself.

The first place I tackled was the kitchen; dirty plates were all over. Don't ask me why, because I had a damn dishwasher. I didn't expect better though, because Hassan was a fucking pig. I then moved on to the living room, which smelled like pure ass. I went to go grab my vacuum when I heard the doorbell ringing. Who the hell was that? *I'm not in the mood for company,* I thought as I walked to the door.

Imani Gibson
The pain was intense. I had cramps in my stomach and lower back. I tried to call out for help, but I was too weak; besides, Josiah had his music blasting. I felt

something wet underneath me and when I put my hands to investigate, I found out it was blood. I reached for my cell phone and dialed 911.

The police banged on the door, terrifying Josiah. He ran into my room yelling, "Mama, the police and ambulance people at the door. Are you aiight?"

"No baby, Mama not feeling too good. Go ahead, let them in."

Minutes later, they were wheeling me out on a stretcher. I could hear Josiah yelling in the background. I wanted to tell my baby it'd be okay, but I was too weak and didn't have the strength. Soon as they got me to the hospital, they rushed me to the second floor to get an ultrasound done. The doctor said he was trying to find my baby's heartbeat and checked to see whether the amniotic sac that surrounded my baby was normal. I kept whispering a silent prayer to God. I didn't want to lose my baby. This might be Hassan's baby.

Shortly after the ultrasound, the doctor entered my room.

"Ms. Gibson, I'm so sorry to inform you that you've had a miscarriage."

"What? Are you sure?"

"Yes ma'am. You're bleeding pretty heavily and there's no sign of a heartbeat. I'm going to perform a D&C, which is a dilation and curettage. Basically, it's a procedure to remove tissue from inside your uterus. This can be painful for you, so I'll put you under a light sedation." Everything around me seemed blank. I couldn't comprehend what this man was saying to me; the only thing I could think about was Hassan. I couldn't lose him and now I had no baby to show him.

"Ms. Gibson, I don't mean to intrude, but looking at how swollen your face is, I have to ask: did someone do something to cause this miscarriage?"

"No, I bumped into the wall."

"I'm going to get you a grief counselor in here to talk with you."

"Grief counselor? Can this bitch bring me back my baby? I doubt it." I looked at the doctor with an attitude.

I woke up feeling kind of out of it, and that's when it hit me: I was no longer pregnant. I rubbed my hand across my stomach. Even though I wasn't far along, I'd known my baby was inside of me. I was hurting so much. "What did I do to deserve this?" I cried out.

"Hello Ms. Gibson. My name is Dr. Aletha Stewart. I'm the grief counselor here at the hospital. I know this might be a stupid question, but I have to ask. How are you feeling today?"

"Have you ever had a miscarriage before?"

"No ma'am, I can't say I have."

"So there's no need to talk to you. Just because you went to school for this shit, don't mean you know what the hell I'm going through."

"I understand, but sometimes talking with a profes-sional can help you get through this difficult time."

"Listen lady, unless you can give me back my baby, I don't have anything to say to you. Please leave me the fuck alone and tell that doctor I'm ready to leave up out of here," I yelled.

I guess she got the picture, because she walked hur-riedly out the room.

I was still feeling weak, but that was only the physical pain. The mental pain of losing my child was killing me softly. To make matters worse, I'd been calling Hassan to tell him I was in the hospital and had lost our baby, but he never picked up the phone and I knew he got my messages. I even called the office, but was told by the new secretary that he was not in. Bullshit. I knew his schedule so I knew he was not in court all day. I guess her ass must've been fucking him also.

My first day out of the hospital was terrible. I was no longer hurting and I was mad as hell. While in the hospital, I learned that I had gonorrhea. I'd been fucking since I was a little girl and I'd never caught anything. This lying ass nigga had the nerve to say I gave that shit to him. Even though I fucked Corey, I strongly doubted he was the one that burned me. I was mad as hell 'cause that nigga could've given me AIDS. This nigga Hassan was playing with my life and I didn't like it one bit.

My tears were no longer flowing as I decided that I was done dealing with his lies and bullshit. I got into my car; I was about to put a stop to this nigga. My thing was that if I couldn't have him, then nobody else needed to have him. Hassan wanted to say fuck me and my child. He had not even bothered to check on my baby while I was gone. That shit was foul. For fifteen years, he sat up here claiming how much he loved my son and all it took was a few moments for him to say fuck him. That showed me that Hassan didn't love him anyway. I knew my son was hurting and I wished I could take the pain away.

I parked on the side, grabbed my purse and got out of my vehicle. My heart was beating quickly as I walked toward the door. I wasn't scared, but I knew going to this door like that could play out in all kinds of different situations. I rang the doorbell and waited, but there was no answer. I rang the doorbell again.

"Who is it?" that bitch hollered.

I didn't respond. I was scared that once I said my name she wouldn't open the door. I realized she wasn't going to open it anyway, so I rang the bell again.

"Who is it?"

"It's Imani."

She opened the door, looking all angry. "What the fuck are you doing, ringing my goddamn doorbell?"

"Listen lady, I'm not here on no bullshit. I just think since we're fucking the same man, we need to talk."

"Talk? What could possibly be the reason for a woman like me to talk to a dirty-ass, home-wrecking bitch? Why are you really here? Is it because he beat yo' ass up?"

"First off, like I said, I ain't come here for no shit. I thought we was woman enough to talk about this shit that Hassan doing to both of us. I don't care 'bout you calling me no names. Shit, he calls you worse than that."

My patience was wearing out with this ho. She really believed that I wanted to be here. Fuck no. This was the bitch that fucked up any kind of future I had with Hassan. I really should've hit her in the fucking face, but I decided to go a different route. That way, I would definitely get Hassan's attention.

CHAPTER TWENTY-ONE

Destiny Clarke

Standing in front of me on my doorstep was Hassan's bitch. Yes, you heard me right: the bitch Imani that claimed she was a secretary had the fucking nerve to ring my doorbell. Soon as I opened the door, I noticed her face was bruised and swollen. I knew then that Hassan had beat her ass up. I wondered what she thought she would get out of coming to my door.

After standing there going back and forth with this home-wrecking ho, I decided that maybe the bitch could benefit me in one way or another.

"Come on in, it's too cold to be standing out here."

I saw the hesitation across her face. "What the hell you looking like that for? You was bold enough to ring my doorbell, so be woman enough to come in here and talk. Ain't that what you want to do?"

"Don't you try nothing 'cause I'm known for busting a bitch in her head." She walked into my house.

I looked around and then locked my door.

"You can sit in here." I walked into the living room.

"So Imani, tell me; how long have you been screwing my husband?"

"Screwing your husband? Lady, Hassan was my man. We'd been dating for years before you came in the picture."

"Is that so? Because I never heard of you or your little bastard before."

"Bastard? Hold up now. I don't play no games when it comes down to my motherfucking child." That ho jumped up and tried to attack me.

"Sit your ass down," I yelled and brought my can of mace from behind me and maced her ass.

"*Aargh*, you stupid bitch. You just maced me."

"Like I said, sit yo' motherfucking ass down. You thought I was a fucking fool when you showed up on my doorstep. See, I know your kind. Little young bitch that thinks pussy alone can hold a fucking man. No, bitch. You need more than good pussy to hold a man."

She got up and I pushed that ho back on the couch. Things were happening so fast, I didn't know what to do; I only knew that this bitch needed to learn a lesson.

"Hassan was right when he said you was a crazy bitch. Move so I can get the fuck out of here."

"You ain't going anywhere until I say so."

I sprayed some more mace in that ho's face.

"Help, help, help, you fucking crazy, bitch. I'ma kill your ass!" she screamed.

I wasn't trying to hear that ho. I ran into my kitchen and grabbed my big frying pan. I walked over to the bitch. She had her head down trying to wipe the mace out of her eyes. I used both hands, lifted the pan up and busted her dead in the head a few times. Blood gushed from the side of her head and the blows knocked that bitch out cold. She fell to the ground.

I checked her vitals; she was still breathing. I stood there looking at her, my heart racing. I thought of calling the police, but I knew better. Going to jail, was definitely not in the plan. I took a deep breath to gather my thoughts . . .

I then went down into the basement where Hassan had some rope. I came back upstairs and tied her legs and her hands together. I then dragged her ass down the stairs to the basement.

Damn, that's one heavy bitch, I thought.

I looked around, but couldn't find any tape. I needed to make a run to the store.

Soon as I got outside, I noticed that her car was parked on the side. *Fuck*, I thought. *Don't panic.* I rushed back inside and grabbed her purse. I dug into it and found the keys. I then walked calmly to her car. I'm happy my neighbors were older people who barely ever came outside. I was astonished to see the bitch was pushing a Lexus—the Lexus that Hassan had bought. I tried to stay calm; this was not the time for me to be getting all emotional and shit. I drove down White Plains Road and pulled up on E 229th Street. This was a residential area, so her vehicle wouldn't seem suspicious. I wiped the steering wheel down and got out. I watched the *Forensic Files* show enough to know not to leave my fingerprints. I got out and walked toward White Plains Road. I walked to the corner of White Plains Road and 229th Street. There was a hardware store across the street. I looked around and saw an old drunk standing around.

"Hey, you, can you go in the store and buy me a roll of duct tape? I got twenty big ones for you."

"Of course, pretty lady," he grinned, showing his dirty teeth.

I stood outside, feeling all different kind of emotions. I'd never broken the law before. Shit, I'd never even got a speeding ticket before. This felt strange because in a matter of minutes, I'd committed more than one felony. *Maybe I should leave*, I thought.

"Here you go, pretty lady. Can I get your number?"

I snatched the tape from him, shoved the twenty dollars in his hand and walked off. I jumped into one of the Livery cabs that was on standby.

"3253 Nereid Avenue."

"Okay ma'am."

He dropped me off at Mama's address. I walked to the door and knocked.

"Who is it?"

"It's me, Mama."

"What's going on? You driving? I thought you was supposed to be resting and where your car is?"

"I didn't drive. I caught a cab over here."

"Come in. You sure you all right? You look pale."

"I'm fine, Mama." I walked into the living room.

"Baby, do you need something to eat?"

"No Mama, I'm good. I need to talk to you."

"Oh, okay, here I come."

"Mama, sit down."

I took her hands into mine and then I looked her in the eyes. "Mama, if anything happens to me I need you to take care of Amaiya."

"Destiny, what are you talking about baby? You're scaring me, what supposed to happen to you? Talk to me!"

"Mama, I loved you from the first day they told me I could go home with you. You're my best friend and my world. There's nothing I wouldn't do for you. But please don't question me because I need to keep you out of this. I just need to know that if anything happens to me you'll take care of my baby." I looked at her with tears in my eyes.

"Baby, you're making me scared. That look in your eyes. Destiny, please talk to me!" she squeezed my hands.

"I love you, but please, answer my damn question. Will you take care of my child if something was to happen to me?"

"Yes, yes, I'll take care of Amaiya," she wept.

"Do me a favor, please."

"Anything. What is it?"

"Pick up your granddaughter from school and let her stay with you until I come get her."

"This don't sound too good, Destiny. I'm worried about you."

"I'm about to call a cab. I love you."

"Nonsense, let me drop you off."

The ride from Mama's house to my house was silent on my part. I was nervous and my mind was racing. I could tell Mama was worried because she kept making small talk with me, but I barely responded. I loved my mama and I needed to protect her. The less she knew, the better it was for her.

She pulled into my driveway and looked at me. "Do you need me to come in? I'll just listen. I won't say a word, baby girl."

I smiled at her and touched her face. "You are my mother and ever since I was a little girl, you've been there caring for me and protecting me. Let me stand on my own feet this time around. Please."

Without saying goodbye, I got out of the car and walked toward my door. I took a deep breath and opened my door.

Let the games begin, I thought as I entered the house.

CHAPTER TWENTY-TWO

Hassan Clarke

"Hello," I answered my phone with an attitude.It was Josiah on the line. He'd been blowing up my phone for a few hours and I had no intention to talk to him. I already told his ass that I wasn't his father and even though it was cutting me deep, there was no way I was going to play daddy to a bastard that wasn't mine.

"Dad, it's me Josiah," his voice crackled through the phone.

"Yo, what's good? I thought I told you the other day, I aint yo' daddy," I sternly said.

"Dad, have you seen ma?"

"Nah, I ain't seen her. I don't deal wit' yo' mama anymore. If she's not there, she might be with that nigga Corey. That's who your daddy is." I was ready to get off the phone.

"Why you being so nasty? I call you to ask you if you've seen my Moms and this is how you act. On the real I don't even know why she fucks with you."

"Nigga, you better watch your mouth. You hear me?" I yelled into the phone.

"Or what, Dad? You goin' beat me the same way you beat on my Moms?"

"Little nigga, don't you forget, I was the one that fed and clothed your ass when yo' ole trifling-ass couldn't do it. You owe me yo' motherfucking life. You hear me? You owe me!" I yelled.

He didn't respond. Instead, he hung up the phone. I was tight as fuck. I wanted to beat that little nigga's ass. Not so much for the shit he did, but for the grimy shit his mama pulled.

I was still heated that Imani's ass played me like that. I was too embarrassed to call my Mama and them. I didn't even know how to let her know that Josiah wasn't her grandchild. I wanted to kill that bitch. It was one thing to play with my fucking feelings, but when you played with my mama's feelings, it got serious. I played a lot of games, but I didn't play when it came down to Mama.

Finding that nigga Corey was a top priority. There was no way I was going to let that nigga get away with what he did to me. I sat in my office pondering how I was going to go about it. I was well aware that I was a lawyer and I didn't want to get my hands dirty. That was when a brilliant idea popped into my head. I grabbed my cell phone and dialed the number to this thug that I defended on a case and got him off. He owed me big time and I recalled him telling me if I ever needed a favor, I should holla at him. Well the time had come for me to call in that favor.

CHAPTER TWENTY-THREE

Destiny Clarke

A woman could go through so many years of pain and abuse, but there came a fucking point in life when enough was enough. I had never been in trouble before, nor did I have a criminal past because trust me, going to prison was not in the equation.

I locked the door and peeped out the side of the window to make sure Mama was gone. I hated to see her go, but there was no way I would involve her in anything illegal. I rushed to the kitchen and poured myself a glass of wine. I drank it in one big gulp. That wasn't enough, so I poured a second and a third glass. I burst out crying. I felt like I was falling apart.

"God, what am I going to do?" I screamed out and fell to my knees.

I held onto the counter and started bawling my heart out. The pain ripped through my soul. I wanted it to all go away: Hassan, his bitch, and all the pain I was feeling. *Damn!* A few seconds later, it hit me that the bitch was in my basement and I needed to get down there fast. I couldn't risk Hassan coming to the house and finding her. I got up, wiped my tears, and grabbed the bag that had the tape inside and ran down the stairs.

I let out a gush of air when I saw she was still there. She was starting to come to and looked at me, as I was walking toward her.

"Bitch, what the fuck you did? I'm going to beat your ass, soon as I get out of here," she barely mumbled.

My heart felt pity for her because she was a woman, like myself, who got caught up in a love triangle with this two-timing ass nigga, Hassan. I wanted to help her, but . . .

"Bitch, untie me," she screamed.

I took another long look at her and decided against it.

"You know little girl, none of this would be happening if you did not talk so much. I get it, you were fucking my husband, but I wouldn't have known if you did not call my phone to brag about it. See, this is the difference between a young bitch and a grown woman. A grown woman would've taken the cock, got paid, and played her position to the fullest. I'm not angry with you because you're nothing but a young, dumb bitch," I spat.

"Bitch, fuck you, Hassan didn't want yo old ass. He loves me, he was only using you for the money. He often complained to me about your old, raggedy ass."

"I'm going to say this, then I'm finish schooling yo' young ass. Hassan is a dog. He will say whatever he needs to say whenever it benefits him. If he loves you like you claim, he wouldn't have busted your face up like that. That is not love, but then again look at you, you're pitiful." I spit in that hoe's face.

She started screaming and hollering. Calling me all kinds of names. That kind of behavior definitely stirred up all the emotions that were bottled up inside of me. I grabbed an axe that was nearby.

"*Ahhhh*," I took a chop at her, but I missed the first time and almost chopped my damn foot.

I think God intervened on her behalf because I was ready to kill that whore. Who the fuck did she think she was, coming up in my shit like this?

"No!" she screamed out and held her head.

I dropped the axe and dropped to my knees. I wrapped my ten, tiny fingers tightly around that whore's neck as I flashbacked to times when my stepfather fucked me as a child. My blood boiled with rage as I remembered the pain I went through. I took out every bit of anger that I felt throughout my life on her ass.

"Please, no! Please," she barely screamed out while gasping for air.

I finally let her neck loose, then touched her pale looking face. I knew if I had continued to squeeze a little longer, I would have ended her life.

"Why couldn't you just leave us alone? I didn't want any trouble. All I wanted was to have my husband, that's all," I said as I wept.

CHAPTER TWENTY-FOUR

Hassan Clarke

I had a meeting with dude named Big Dre. He was the dude that I got off on a murder rap a few months ago. He didn't hesitate when I told him I needed a favor. I was cautious not to discuss business over the phone. See I wasn't a fool. I knew that dude was already hot and I couldn't risk getting torn off with this career criminal.

I opened the safe in my office. Even though we hadn't decided on a price, I wanted to give this nigga a down payment. I took out two grand, closed the safe, and walked out of the office.

"Hey, Shari, I'm leaving for the remainder of the day. Please forward all calls to my cell."

"Okay, boss. Will do. You have a good one."

I nodded at her and then walked out the door. Damn, the sound of her Trinidadian accent sent chills through my dick, which gave me an instant erection. Funny thing was that I'd had my eyes set on her since the first day she walked into the office and applied for the job. I peeped she was the kind that like to play hard to get. She just didn't know that was my type because I would punish that pussy just because she played hard to get. I had a strong feeling I was going to be banging her back out pretty soon.

***

I carefully parked on the side of building far away from the cameras. I noticed his Charger was parked to the far right. I walked up to the car and got inside.

"Whaddup Bossman?"

"I can't call it. Things kind of crazy right now."

"Oh yea? So what can I help you with?"

"Before I start, I need to know that you aren't wearing no wire or no shit like that."

"What you just say to me nigga? Do I look like a motherfucking rat? He snapped.

"Nah, chill dawg. I ain't mean nothing like that. I'm a lawyer so you can understand why I have to be careful." I tried to diffuse the situation quickly.

"Aiight yo, what kind of favor do you need? Make it quick, I got shit to do."

I wasn't feeling this nigga's attitude. This bum must've forgotten who got him acquitted of all charges, and if I hadn't gotten him off, he would've been in prison probably getting fucked in the ass. He had no idea he owed me his motherfucking freedom.

"Yo, I don't know if you remember a nigga named Corey from over in Edenwald. He used to be with me, back in the day. Anyways, I got word that he hangs out at Big Len auto body in Mount Vernon. The nigga violated me when he fucked my baby mama and I need him handled."

"Ha ha, so lemme get this right. You want me to fuck up a nigga over a bitch? Damn my nigga, I thought you was a G." He stared at me.

"Watch your mouth. That bitch belongs to me, and that nigga was my right hand man."

I wanted to punch this dude in the throat, but I didn't 'cause I peeped the 9mm Glock on the mat by his feet. I was his lawyer, so I was aware that he was a cold-blooded killer.

"Aiight yo, give me e'erything you got on the nigga. So lemme get this right. You want me to rough him up a little or you want me to body him?"

"Don't leave no witnesses. I need him to pay for the bullshit he pulled. Here's two grand. Take it as a down payment. When the job is complete, you can tell me how much I owe you. I need this to remain between us, you understand? I can't afford to have my name associated with anything illegal." I looked him dead in the eyes.

"Man, keep that chump change. I gotcha, but I need you to understand if I ever get into another jam, the tab will be on you."

"Here is a picture of dude. It's a little old, but trust me, he still looks the same."

He snatched the picture out of my hand. "Aiight yo, got to go."

I didn't say another word. I opened the car door and stepped out into the brisk air. I nervously walked away from his car. I expected to see law enforcement rushing in from all angles. I guess I'd seen too many murder-for-hire cases where the person that is being hired is not a killer, but a police detective. I braced the cold and headed to my car. I got inside, sat down, and let out a long sigh. I took a quick look around before I pulled off.

I pulled into my driveway and took a deep breath. I hated coming to the house; just the sight of that bitch made me sick to my stomach. I could've found me another place to live, but there was no way I was going let this bitch think she could put me out my shit. I wouldn't put a dollar into buying the house, but I was married to the bitch, so technically what was hers was ours and what was mine was motherfucking mine. Bottom line was, I wasn't going anywhere until I was motherfucking ready.

Soon as I stepped foot into the door and took my shoes off, I looked up and here this bitch was, standing in front of me with an axe in her hand. She looked deranged, like a bitch in hell. Her eyes widened as she took a step toward me.

"I told you I want you out of my shit!" she yelled.

"Yo B, go ahead on. I ain't stuttin' yo ass." I pushed her away from me.

She looked at me and smiled. It wasn't a friendly smile. It was more like a devilish grin. This was the first time I'd ever seen her behave like this. The woman that I knew was fragile and scared. This bitch that stood in front of me looked cold and unhinged.

"Aye yo, Destiny, I ain't goin' nowhere 'til I'm ready. You need to put that axe down before you do something stupid. I thought you would've learned not to fuck wit' me after what happened to you last time."

"Fuck you, you dirty bastard. I gave you too many chances, but you done ran out. You disgust me, running around here like you're god's blessing to women. You and that ole, filthy ass cock. You make my fucking soul sick and to think I fucking loved you. I should've left your dirty ass a long time ago."

I was sick of hearing her mouth. I dropped my briefcase, then took a step toward her, and slapped her face back to back.

She stepped closer, raised the axe and cut me on my arm, twice.

"You crazy bitch! You just fucking cut me. I'm going to beat your motherfucking ass."

I tried to grab at her, but the pain was intense and blood was dripping everywhere. She stood there with the axe raised with an evil look plastered across her face.

"Come closer, so I can get your ass again," she warned.

"Bitch, fuck you. You better watch your motherfucking back."

"I done told yo' ass, get the fuck out of my house or the next time I will go for your head. You hear me, Hassan?"

I picked up my briefcase, put my shoes back on and walked back out the door. *I need to stop this bleeding,* I thought. I got back into my car. I thought about going to the hospital, but decided against it. I didn't want to get the police involved.

I decided to go to my Mama's crib. She always had bandages and knew how to wrap up a wound. I took off my jacket and wrapped it around the open cut, which was pretty deep. The sight of the blood only made me angrier. I wanted to kill that bitch!

I pulled up at Mama's crib on Barnes Avenue. I parked, jumped out the car, and rang the doorbell.

"Who is it?" she hollered.

"It's me, Mama."

She opened the door, and looked at me, like I didn't belong there.

"What a surprise, this is. What's this, the second time since we moved here that you've shown your face? Wait, is that blood dripping? What's wrong wit' your arm?" she became concerned.

I walked past her and into the kitchen. "Mama, I need you to clean this for me and dress it up."

"Boy, what the hell done happened? Who did this to you?" She took the jacket from around my arm.

"Man, that crazy bitch cut me with an axe."

"Say what? What crazy bitch and did you call the police on her ass?" she asked as she poured peroxide into my open wound.

"Destiny, ole, dumb ass. Nah, I ain't call the police. Shit, half the force in the Bronx knows me and I don't want my business out there."

"I'm going to call Charmaine when I'm finish. You know she 'ont play when it comes down to you. I told yo' ass to leave that old, trifling ass bitch alone, but you too damn hard-headed. Oh shoot! I almost forgot to ask you. Have you seen Imani? Josiah been looking for his mama."

"Nah, he called my phone, but I told him I ain't seen her. So, he still can't find her? I mean, even though she a ho, that ain't like her to not let her son know where she at."

"Boy, watch your mouth! Imani is a good woman. I wish you would see that and quit playing with that girl's feelings."

I looked at her as she spoke with such conviction. She had no idea the type of woman Imani really was. It hurt my heart that she even had my Mama fooled. There was no easy way to let it be known, but I had to tell her.

After she finished bandaging up my wound, she gave me two painkillers. Ever since we were young, she was good with playing Dr. Mom. Here I was, a grown ass man, still having my Mama playing doctor. I was feeling all sorts of emotions. Now everybody was going to be up in my business all because of that bitch.

She walked into the kitchen. I heard her on the phone. I figured she was talking to my little sister Charmaine. She was my ride or die. I knew all hell was about to break loose. Mama walked into the living room where I was seated. My arm was throbbing and my blood was boiling. I couldn't stop thinking of all the things that I wanted to do to that ho.

"Hey bro," Charmaine interrupted my thoughts.

"What's up, li'l sis?"

"Yo! What the fuck Mama talking 'bout that bitch Destiny cut you?"

"Yea man, me and that ho got into it and that stupid bitch grabbed an axe and cut me on my motherfuck-ing arm."

"And you ain't kill that bitch? Yo, on my Mama's life, I'm gonna beat that bitch up. I 'ont play when it comes down to my motherfucking brother, that ho just don't know. For real bro, I'm kind of happy you didn't do anything stupid though. Let me handle that ho."

Before I could respond Mama walked into the room. I knew this was the time.

"Mama, you and Charmaine need to sit down. I need to talk to y'all."

"Boy what is it? " Mama asked.

"Ok, this ain't the time, but I'ma go ahead and let y'all know Josiah is not my son."

"What? Bro, I know you upset and all, but don't play like that. Josiah is your son. That bitch daughter is the one you should question."

"Little sis, I know that's your homegirl and all, but she a ho. I found out she was fucking Corey and Josiah is his son. They both admitted it the other day."

"What? Wait, I remember I told you a few years ago that there was a rumor going around that Corey was tryna mess with Imani. I tried to tell you, but you blew me off. Oh my God, that bitch. She's my fucking friend." Charmaine busted out crying.

"Hassan, I hope you're not saying this because you're upset with her," Mama said, with her eyes filled with tears.

I was genuinely hurt because I could see the pain in their faces, and I knew how much they cared for Josiah. That made my hatred for Imani deeper. She had no idea what pain she had bestowed upon me and my family.

"Listen, I know y'all hurting and shit, but I had to let it out. I couldn't allow y'all to continue investing emotions and money into a little bastard that don't share the same DNA as us. That bitch foul for that shit, though."

I looked at Charmaine; I could see she wasn't taking it too well. She and Imani been best friends for a long time and she had no idea Josiah was not her nephew.

"Sis, come here." I walked over to her and hugged her.

Surprisingly, she pushed me off. "Nah bro, this is fucked up. I rode for that bitch and this is how she repays me? I thought you were the dog and I always let that bitch know e'erything that you were doing and she made a fool out of me."

I looked at her, "What the fuck you mean you let her know what I was doing?"

"Y'all stop it. Y'all hurting," Mama yelled.

"Nah Mama, I want to know what she meant. Charmaine, what the hell you mean?"

"Boy don't be yelling at me. I used to let that bitch know what was going on with you and Destiny. I honestly thought you was the one that was dogging her out. I had no idea she was really messing with Corey." She bawled.

I was disgusted by what my sister was saying to me. Now it all made sense. I used to wonder how Imani knew a lot of things. I had no idea my little sister would betray me like this.

I looked at her, then at Mama. "That's fucked up. You're my little sister, my blood, and this how you do me?"

"Hassan, whatever! You're just like daddy! You want to have your cake and eat it too. She was my friend! I didn't like how you was treating her and then you turned around and married that stupid ass bitch that disrespected your whole family. Don't sit up here acting like you're a victim. If you really want to know, I think you deserve all this shit," she spat.

"Charmaine, that's your big brother. Don't talk to him like that."

"No Mama, I'm tired of this shit. I see the way daddy treats you. He is just like Daddy," she said and stormed out the door.

"I'm sorry that this has happened to you. I know how much you loved that boy." Mama gave me a hug.

No matter what went down, I could always count on Mama to have my back and that was why she would always be the number one woman in my life.

"So back to that heffa, Destiny. You need to get rid of her ass, soon as possible. I told you that bitch was out for herself, now you see. You need to file for divorce and get a blood test on that little girl. Don't play no fool for these bitches. You a good man and you deserve better."

Mama had no idea how much I needed to hear those words. The past weeks had been crazy and I just needed to know that I had her in my corner. "I'm done with her ass, and I don't give a fuck if Amaiya is my seed, she can have her. I don't need the headache at all. I'm done."

CHAPTER TWENY-FIVE

Destiny Clarke

Hassan wouldn't quit. I told his ass to leave my house and instead of going away, he stuck around to terrorize me. I was no longer scared of him, but more scared of what he might force me to do.

I walked into my doctor's office earlier to get my results and do a follow up visit. As usual, I was nervous and scared that this wasn't the end of it. The bastard already had my pussy on fire and smelling like fish.

"Good morning Mrs. Clarke. Dr. Li Yung is running a little late. Take a seat please."

"Good morning, thank you."

I flopped down in the chair. I was feeling the same way I felt before. I tried to calm myself down because it wasn't that long ago I'd had a heart attack over this same bull-shit. I was also aware that herpes couldn't be cured. Lord help this nigga if he gave me some shit that I couldn't get rid of. I sat there looking into space and shaking my legs. I was trying to calm my nerves.

"Good morning Mrs. Clarke," Dr. Li Yung startled me.

I smiled at him, and then mumbled, "Good morning,"

"Please come with me. How are you feeling this morning?"

"Well, I'm feeling a little better. Sometimes I get light-headed and I also get tired easily."

"All right, listen to me: I need you to avoid putting stress on your body. You were fortunate the first time when you had that heart attack, but that doesn't mean you're in the clear. It might be a major heart attack the next time around, if you do have one. Take a break from everything and relax."

"I understand doc." I smiled at him.

After he examined me, he asked me to go back out to the waiting area.

I tried to pay attention to the Queen Latifah Show on the television, but my mind was all over the place and the words that were coming from the television were not registering.

I was so caught up in my thoughts I didn't see when the nurse returned. "Mrs. Clarke? Come with me," she said.

I followed her into Dr. Li Yung's office.

"Have a seat Mrs. Clarke." He turned to face me, took off his glasses, then spoke.

My heart started racing even before any words came out his mouth.

"Well, I have good news and bad news. The good news is your follow-up tests are negative. You no longer have the gonorrhea or the trichomoniasis."

"What about the herpes?" I asked, cutting him off.

"I'm sorry, Mrs. Clarke, but you've tested positive for herpes."

"Are you sure?" I barely mumbled.

Deep down I heard what he said, but I still had to be sure.

"Yes, the test came back positive for genital herpes. Genital herpes is common and highly contagious. This infection is usually caused by the herpes simplex virus-2, HSV-2, or the herpes simplex virus-1, HSV-1, the virus that is usually responsible for cold sores. It can't be cured, but we have medicines that can suppress the virus and prevent outbreaks."

I was a nurse goddammit. Everything he was telling me, I already knew. My lips trembled as tears filled my eyes. I tried not to cry, but I couldn't. My heart was hurting. This bum not only gave me trich and gonorrhea, but he also gave me some shit that can't be cured.

"Mrs. Clarke, you are one strong woman, so I know you will pull through all of this. I am going to prescribe Valacyclovir, also known as Valtrex. This won't cure it, but it will reduce the number of outbreaks and also help with the sores or blisters."

"Ok," I said. I didn't have any other words.

"Take care of yourself," he said, smiling and handing me a prescription paper, before he walked out of the room.

I got up out the chair and walked out.

"Have a good day," the receptionist said.

As I walked out, tears started falling. I took a long breath trying to stop myself from breaking down. I walked in a daze to my car and opened the door. I sat there for a second breathing hard, then I pulled off. I wiped my face because I was tired of crying.

After days of crying and praying and asking God for guidance, I decided not to kill this bitch. Believe me, I wasn't a killer and I couldn't put my Mama and my daughter through no drama. I knew damn well I would be gone for life if I committed murder.

It was day five and I had to act fast. I stayed in bed until I heard Hassan's car pulled off. I hated that I had to sneak around in my own fucking house, but I was waiting on my lawyer to file the papers.

I walked over to the door and made sure it was locked. I stopped in the kitchen and made some Ramen noodles, then I took it downstairs.

"Wake your ass up." I shook her.

She opened her eyes, saw it was me and close them back.

"I brought you something to eat."

"Bitch, fuck you, I done told yo ass I ain't hungry. If you goin' kill me, go ahead and do it, 'cause if you don't and I get out of here, I'm goin' kill your motherfucking ass. You hear me?" she yelled.

"Shut up already." I punched her in the face, soon as she turned her head to look at me.

This time she didn't scream, she just sat there staring at me, with her face balled up.

"You know Imani, I'm trying to help yo ass for real, but you are too young and dumb to see that. I could've killed you, 'cause believe I done thought about it, but I didn't because as much I hate yo ass for the pain you brought to my life, I can't really put all the blame on you. I have to blame that sorry ass nigga that I called my husband."

"How you trying to help me? By kidnapping me and feeding me fucking Ramen Noodles. I ain't shower in days and my fucking son must be losing his mind, looking for his mama," she cried.

Damn, I never thought about the little bastard, until she mentioned him.

"Well you have no one to blame, but yourself. Instead of playing mommy to the little monkey, you was over here chasing a cock that doesn't belong to you. Bitch you need to accept some of this blame. As long as there are bitches like you who enable these no good ass niggas, they will continue to treat us good women wrong."

"You know what Destiny? I had enough of your fucking preaching. All that self-righteous shit you talking is not goin' make Hassan love you or stay faithful to you. So bitch, let's get to the point: what is it you want from me?" she yelled.

I was happy no one else was home because this dumb ass bitch was really showing her ass. I thought she would have never asked. I learned a long time ago that if you couldn't fight these hoes, it was best you joined them. I had the perfect plan in mind. I just hoped that it didn't backfire on me because the fact was that this ho couldn't be trusted.

Imani Gibson

A bitch like me grew up in the South Bronx and I'd had plenty fights growing up. Bitches in my neighborhood knew not to fuck with me because I was beast with my hands. I have never lost a fight and had no intention on losing one now.

This was the main reason why I was in my fucking feelings. I had no idea this bitch had it in her to try some slick shit. The way Hassan described her, I thought she was some scared-ass, bougie bitch from the country. I didn't see anything wrong when she invited me inside and the whole time, I had it in my head how I was gonna beat her down once I got inside.

I didn't see it coming when that bitch sprayed me with mace and I was definitely caught off guard when she hit me upside the head. All I knew at that moment was that I was scared for my life. I had no idea what was going through the bitch's mind. I saw the desperation in her eyes and to be honest, I was scared this bitch would kill me.

"God, please protect me, I can't die. My son needs me," I whispered a silent prayer as tears flowed from my eyes.

I wasn't sure what time of the day it was. Later that day, when I woke up she had me tied up in what seemed like a basement. I thought of trying to escape, but my hands and feet were tied together. I wanted to rip this bitch's neck off her body. I hoped Hassan would show up and show this bitch who he really loved, but it was wishful thinking because that nigga didn't show up.

After days of laying on the concrete floor, my body started to ache. I drank the water she fed me, but refused to eat the noodles. I didn't eat that shit at home and damn sure wasn't going to start eating them now. I prayed that my son would go to the police and report that I was missing and hopefully they would have some sense to come up in here and search.

That hope soon diminished and my anger turned to fear. Each time she approached me, I dreaded it was my last moment. This bitch looked like a sociopath that could snap at any given moment. I tried most of the time to remain calm because I didn't want to trigger her anger. The last time that I said some fucked shit to her, that bitch hit me in my face. In my mind, I was on survival mode and was willing to do any and everything to get out of this fucked up situation that I had managed to get myself into.

"Sit up." She pulled me up.

"What the hell you want now?"

"Sit up and shut up. You need to learn to shut the fuck up sometimes."

I didn't say anything, I just shot that bitch a dirty look. *Ho, I'm going to beat the brakes off you,* I thought.

"All right this is it. I understand that you're in love with my husband and you want me out of the picture, but let me break it down for you honey. I'm going to file for divorce and I'm going to take everything. Yes you heard me right. Everything. When I'm done with that lowlife piece of shit, the only thing he's going to have left is the dirty drawers on his ass. Now this is it: you need to decide who you rolling with."

"What the fuck you mean, who I'm rolling with? Hassan is my man and my loyalty is to him."

"Listen to me little bitch, stop thinking like a dummy. You're young and you have a child. I am offering you a way to get on your feet and get away from this two-timing ass nigga. Don't be stupid. Good cock and loyalty don't pay no bills, you hear me?"

I swear I wasn't trying to fall into this bitch's web of deceit. Here she had me tied up and she really believed that I was going to trust a word that came out of her mouth. I didn't say anything; I played along with her ass. That was until she made me an offer that I couldn't refuse.

I first behaved like I wasn't interested, but I finally gave in after she continued to coerce me,. I was very desperate to get up out of here and get back to my baby. She thought she was playing me, but I was focused on the bigger picture.

CHAPTER TWENTY-SIX

Hassan Clarke

I was nervous as I waited patiently to get news on that nigga Corey. I couldn't sleep because of that shit that he and Imani pulled. I was angry with myself; all these years I had been taking care of a seed that wasn't mine. Somebody had to pay."Mr. Clarke, the police are here to see you." Shari buzzed in.

My eyes popped open. The police? What in God's name would the police want with me ? Oh hell nah, I hope it wasn't about Corey.

"My God," I mumbled.

"Tell them I'm on my way out."

I got up from behind the desk. My legs trembled as I walked out of my office. I saw two white police officers standing in the waiting area. My first instinct was to run, but there was nowhere to escape to.

"Good morning officers. I'm Attorney at Law Hassan Clarke. How may I help you officers?"

"Can we step into your office?"

Shit, this had to be serious, I thought.

"Follow me, gentlemen." I walked into my office.

I took a seat at my desk. "What is this about?"

"Well, we're here because a missing report was filed for one Imani Gibson and we were told that you and her had some kind of personal relationship. We were wondering if you have any idea where she might be?"

"Ms. Gibson and I dated for a brief moment, but I haven't seen or talked to her in over a month. So the answer would be no, I have no idea where she might be."

"Do you know any of her friends or family that she might be with?"

"No, I do not. We were only sleeping together and I've never met any family members. I'm afraid that I can't help you guys. If you all will excuse me, I have a meeting that I have to prepare for."

I got up and walked toward the door, opening it up.

"Well, here's my card. If you hear from her or if you remember anything, please don't hesitate to call."

"Sure." I took the card out of his hand.

I stood at the door as they both walked out of the office.

After they were out of sight, I walked back into my office and shut the door. I took a long breath and sat down in my chair. I tried to bring my anxiety level back down to normal. I just knew my life was over when I heard that the police was here.

The rest of the day at the office was spent in a daze. At first I thought Imani might be shacked up with that nigga Corey's ass, but it seemed to be more serious since the police were involved. I was angry with her and had said some fucked up shit, but I prayed to God nothing foul was wrong with her. Deep down I was still in love with her and I needed to find her.

That evening I left work a little bit earlier so I could stop by her apartment. I rang the doorbell and waited. I was hoping that Josiah was home and could shed some light on the situation. Deep down I knew that Imani would not have left him alone. There was no answer, so I turned to walk away, but right then, the door opened.

"What do you want?" Josiah stood in the doorway.

"Did you hear from your mom?"

"Why? When I called you a few days ago, you acted like you didn't care. Shit, for all I know you could've done something to her."

"Yo, you better chill out little man. You should be careful, throwing accusations around like that."

"Yo I ain't no little man and I say what I want to say. First you beat her up and now she's missing. You're the lawyer. I say that's evidence."

I took a few steps toward him and punched him in the face. "Watch your motherfucking mouth, little nigga." He grabbed me and tried to flip me. We ended up tussling on the ground.

"Stop it, get off him." A woman ran out of the apartment and over to us.

"Who the fuck are you?"

"I'm Imani's cousin. I came over when Josiah called to let me know my cousin hasn't been home in days. And you are?"

"This the nigga that beat her up the other day. My so-called sperm donor," he spat and got up off the ground.

"I'm Hassan. The police came to my office today so I decided to stop by to ask this little dude if he had any idea where his moms might be."

I stood to my feet, loosened my tie, and gritted on Josiah.

"Well, all this ain't called for. I haven't heard from my cousin and this ain't like her to just up and disappear. I just hope she's all right because Josiah needs his mama."

"Yo, it was a mistake for me to come over here." I walked off.

Truth was I was hoping Imani might've come home by now. I had no intention to get into it with his ass, but lately that little nigga was being mad disrespectful and I was not going to tolerate it.

He got me real good when he punched me in my lip. I touched it to make sure it wasn't busted. A saw a little spot of blood so I used my hand to wipe it off then bit down hard on it. If this nigga didn't straighten up, I'd show his young ass that I'm a grown ass man. I got in my car and drove off. Imani was weighing heavily on my mind. *Where are you?* I thought to myself.

CHAPTER TWENTY-SEVEN

Destiny Clarke

You could call me a fool for letting this bitch stay alive, but after spending days praying and asking for guidance, the only option I had was to let her go. Hassan was a two-timing ass and a son of a bitch, and I had too much going for myself to risk going to prison over him and his dirty ass cock.

I knew I risked going to prison for kidnapping if that whore decided to go the police. However, I did know her ass was money hungry and I gave her an offer she couldn't refuse. I gave her ten grand up front if she would help me. At first she laughed in my face like I was a joke, but being the money hungry whore she was, she finally saw things my way.

"I hope I can trust that you won't tell anyone about this. I will give you another forty grand after everything is over and done with. It's enough money to get you and your son back on y'all feet."

"Sure, but how do I know I can trust you?"

"I guess we will never know right. I feel like together we can get a lot accomplished. You don't need his ass. The way I see it, he's already replaced us with that white bitch."

"You know about her?" she quizzed.

"Yea. I know about all the bitches he's been fucking. That's why I don't know which one of y'all burned his ass. When you get out of here, you better go get your ass checked out."

She didn't respond, she just sat there staring at me. I could see she was heartbroken by the information I just fed her ass. I wanted to laugh at this silly bitch; she had no idea that the way she got him was the same way she would lose him. I smiled at her and said, "Listen, I'm about to untie the rope. Please don't make me regret this."

I untied the rope and helped her to her feet. A raw stench hit my nose and I covered it with my hand.

"You need to take a shower ASAP. That pussy of yours is stinking. Hold on."

I walked to the top of the stairs and looked around. I had to make sure the house was empty. Lord knows the last thing I needed was to have Hassan pop up on me.

"Come on up here." I motioned to her.

I waited until she got to the top of the stairs, then I walked upstairs.

"Where are we going?"

"You need to wash your ass. Ain't no way you goin' sit down in my car with your shit smelling like that."

I walked over to the spare bathroom upstairs. There was no way I was going to let that bitch wash her ass in the same tub I bathed in.

I handed her a bar of soap and a washcloth. After I was sure she was bathing, I went to my room and grabbed a new pair of Victoria Secret underwear. I then looked through my closet for a jogging suit that I hadn't worn yet. I didn't think this bitch was worthy to put her ass in anything that I owned.

After she washed her ass and looked halfway decent. I decided to take her to where her ride was parked. On the ride there, she was quiet. I was really worried that this bitch might back out on me and go to the police.

"Aye, you quiet over there. Are you aiight?"

"Aiight? I've been kidnapped for days, and you think I'm aiight. Lady, after all this is over with, I want you out of my life for good. You hear me?"

"I already told you what I want. I don't want to be your fucking friend. You need to be careful of everything that you do. Hassan is far from being a fool and by the look of your face the other day, you know what he is capable of doing too." I looked at her with a serious face.

When we got to the location where I parked her cross-over, it wasn't there.

"Where is my shit at?" she yelled.

"Relax. It might've gotten towed. You need to call around and find out. Here's the money that I promised. You will get the rest later, as agreed."

She looked at me and turned her head.

"I'm about to drop you off at home. I'm pretty sure they were looking for you. Please have your story straight. You know how to make up a believable story? Just tell them you needed a break."

"You ain't got to tell me what to say. I got this. Don't think for a minute I like yo ass. I'm not doing this to help you. I'm doing this because that bastard played me and left me for dead."

"That will work."

I pulled up at the address that I caught Hassan.

"Here you go, give me your number and I will contact you in a few days. I don't have to tell you to keep this between us."

She gave me the number, and I put it into my phone. She got out of the car without saying another word.

I didn't hang around and pulled off. I was nervous, but confident that she would keep her word. Not because I thought that whore was loyal, but because I knew she was hurt and like me, she was determined to take his ass down for her own reasons. I didn't care what her motives were. I needed all the help that I could get.

***

After I dropped her off, I decided to swing by Mama's house. It'd been days since I'd seen my baby girl. I didn't want her at the house because at the time I had no idea how the situation was going to play out. Mama knew something was up and she kept calling to check up on me, or so she said. I knew she was worried about me and I hated that I had to put her through this. She didn't understand, but if that bitch decided to go to the police, I'd be the only one she could implicate in the situation.

I pulled up and got out. I was still feeling nervous from all the things that had happened the last few days. I looked around to make sure the police weren't following me. I rang the doorbell and waited. A few seconds later, Mama opened the door.

"I almost didn't answer the door. What happen to calling before you come over?"

"You're my Mother so that don't apply to me. Furthermore, my child is here," I joked and walked past her.

"Mama, Mama." Amaiya ran over to me.

"Hey baby." I kissed her on the cheek.

"Can I come home now? I love it here with grandma, but I miss being in my own space."

"Yes, you can come home."

"The last time I saw you, you were acting all kind of crazy. What changed from then until now?" Mama asked.

"Mama, I told you the other day that I can't bring you into this and that still stands. I need you to trust me on this," I said in an annoyed tone.

I knew she meant well, but I already told her that I didn't want to involve her in anything.

"Did you talk to that lawyer? Don't you sit over there and listen to his foolishness. Long as you keep taking him back and putting up with his foolishness, that man ain't goin' change his ways."

"Mama, I hear you loud and clear. Ain't nobody falling for his foolishness. I haven't talked to that man at all. Trust me, I'm sick and tired of being hurt and I really am ready to move on with my life."

I got up and walked into the kitchen, where Amaiya was. "Get your stuff together so we can go."

Mama walked in behind me, "Destiny I didn't mean to make you upset. You're my child and I'm tired of seeing you hurt." She started crying.

I stepped closer to her and hugged her. "Come here, Mama. I'm not upset with you, I just want all this to be over already. I want to move on with my life, you know?"

I started to cry and we both stood there hugging each other tight. I wish I hadn't put her through this, but it was already happening and all I could do was try to change it.

"Mama, I'm ready." Amaiya walked in.

I let Mama go and quickly wiped my tears. I hated for Amaiya to see us going through this.

"All right, we're about to go. Love you. I'll call you tomorrow."

"Bye Nana. Love you."

I held my daughter's hand and we walked out of the house and into my car. The entire ride home was completely silent. My mind was still on Imani and not knowing if she'd gone to the police or not.

"Mama, you okay? You keep looking in your rearview mirror."

"Uh, yeah I'm fine, baby. It's just a bad habit," I lied.

She had no idea how nervous her mama really was. The thought of getting cuffed in front of my child really scared me.

Imani Gibson
Everybody I knew had a whole bunch of questions as to where I'd been for the past few days. I couldn't really

tell them the crazy shit that Hassan's bitch kidnapped me and held me hostage in her basement. This was the kind of thing you'd see on Law and Order or Criminal Minds, on TV shows.

I was happy to be back home with my son. I didn't care what I was going through in life; I never wanted to be without him. Tears filled my eyes as I rubbed my stomach. Hatred filled my soul as I remembered losing my baby. The funny thing about it was that I still loved Hassan. Even after all that he had done to me.

Most would call me stupid because I took the ten grand from Destiny. But I begged to differ. If that bitch had that kind of loot sitting around, shit, why shouldn't I take it? After all the stress she done put me through, the bitch owed me. I lay in bed contemplating if I should go to the police and have her arrested. Shit, that would get her out of the picture for good and then maybe Hassan and I could live happily ever after. Right, I thought, but there was the white bitch Tanya; I had to get rid of her ass, too.

"You dog," I yelled out.

I woke up in an upbeat mood. I was happy that I was finally back in my own space. I got my ride from the pound and closely inspected it—there were no visible scratches on my baby. I checked my cell phone and noticed I had a million and one messages. There were a ton of messages from Corey, some from Hassan, and from the police department. I didn't bother to listen to Corey's messages. Whatever that nigga had to say was of no interest to me. I was done with him; I was caught up in all this shit with Hassan because of him. Next, I listened to Hassan's messages. Truth be told, they were not the regular mean messages; these ones were kind and warm. He even mentioned that he loved and missed me. I smiled as I listened to his voice through the phone.

It was strange though since just the other day he wanted to kill me, but I now that I'd been gone for a few days he suddenly loved and missed me. I almost fell for that shit too, until I remembered that he spat in my face.

Hassan's mother left me a message saying that she wanted to see me and Josiah. I knew she must've been worried out of her mind. I decided to roll over there to see how they were doing. I pulled up and parked on the side. I rang the doorbell and no one answered. I looked back and saw Charmaine's car parked on the opposite side so I knew they were home. I rang the doorbell again. This time Ms. Paulette yelled, "Who is it?"

"It's me, Imani," I happily said.

The door opened and his mother stood in the doorway with an angry look plastered across her face, but I didn't think anything about it."Hey Ms. Paulette." I stepped past her.

"Who the hell is that Ma?" Charmaine hollered from upstairs.

"Girl, it's me," I said, walking toward the step.

Charmaine ran down the stairs and got into my face. "Bitch, I can't believe you have the nerve to show yo' face 'round here."

"Bitch, what you talking 'bout? I just needed a little time to myself, you know?"

"I 'ont care about yo ass disappearing and shit. I'm talking 'bout how you lie that Josiah was my brother's baby and all along you knew it was that lame-ass nigga Corey's baby." She uppercut me.

I didn't hesitate. I grabbed that bitch's weave and pulled her down to the ground.

"Get off my child. You won't come up in here putting your hand on my damn baby," Ms. Paulette said as she started punching me.

I tried to fight back, but Hassan's mama was a big bitch and was good at throwing those big ass hands. I continued pulling Charmaine's hair and tried to throw a few punches at the same time. I was determined not to get beat down so I scratched as hard as I could.

"You stupid bitch, get off of me." I dug my nails into that bitch's face. I was wanted to draw blood.

Somehow, we managed to separate. I was out of breath and my head was hurting; one of these stupid bitches had pulled out my freshly glued-in Remy weave. I looked on the ground and saw a patch of my hair on the carpet. I was furious and even though I was tired, I wanted to go another round.

"Get out of my motherfucking house you lying-ass bitch. I fucking defended you all these years and cussed my brother out over you when all along you was fucking playing. Get out!" Charmaine screamed.

I wanted to say, "Nah bitch, put me out," but instead I straightened my clothes and limped out of the house.

I got into my ride feeling hurt as fuck. These people were like family to me and in a split second they turned against me, attacking me like I was a bitch in the streets. I couldn't fucking understand it and I was pissed to the max. I wondered who the hell told them Josiah was not Hassan's child. Only three of us knew about this, and I know damn well I didn't tell anyone. The only two people left were Corey and Hassan.

My body was aching from the pressure of that bitch's humongous body. I looked in my mirror and noticed my lip was busted. I took another look at the house and pulled off. I made a mental note to catch each one of them bitches by themselves.

I ran upstairs and quickly opened the door. I knew I looked a hot mess and didn't want anyone of these nosy bitches to see me like that.

"Mama, you aiight?" Josiah startled me.

I turned around, "Yes baby, I'm good."

"W-h-a-t, wrong wit' you face? Did that nigga hit you again?"

"Boy no, and what I tell you 'bout talking 'bout yo' daddy like that? Show him some respect." I was annoyed.

My head was thumping and I was mad as fuck, now wasn't the time for this.

"Josiah, listen I'm not feeling good and I don't feel like fighting."

"Ma, why are you always defending this nigga? I swear if I find out he's the one that hit you, I put this on my life, I'm going to murk his ass."

I slapped his face hard.

"Don't you ever raise your voice at me and stay out of grown folks business. You hear me?"

"Yea, until his ass kill you. I can't believe you." He looked at me with pity in his eyes. Without saying another word, he walked away.

I ran into my room and up under my covers. *Fuck my life*, I thought.

CHAPTER TWENTY-EIGHT

Hassan Clarke

Mama called me to tell me how Imani came over there and jumped on her. I had mixed feelings. I was mad—she put her hands on my Moms—but I was also happy that they found her. I couldn't get her off my mind and I had feared the worst. I told her I would handle Imani, which was true, but I had questions of my own. I wanted to know where the hell she'd been hiding.

I picked up my cell and dialed her number.

"Hello," she barely answered.

"Aye yo, what's good?"

"Ain't nothing good."

There was a long pause. I wanted to confront her about the shit that happened between her and Mama, but I knew this might not be the best route to take. It wasn't like we'd been on good terms and I didn't want to push it too soon. In due time, I would make sure she knew it was a no-no. I didn't play that shit. I didn't care what the fuck my Moms did, I didn't want a nigga or a bitch to ever raise their hands to her.

"How you been? I'm happy to know you're back."

"I'm good. And you?"

Hmm, her attitude kind of threw me off. I expected her to be upset and cussing me out. I recalled that the last time I saw her was when I beat her up.

"I'm straight, ma. I was wondering if we could have lunch or something."

"I 'ont know 'bout all that. Let me get back to you."

"I understand. Well, you got my number. Hit my line and let me know what you decide."

"Okay, sure will." She hung the phone up.

I had no idea why I was still trying to see her ass. Truth was the bitch played me in the worst way, but I couldn't stop thinking about her. I missed fucking her and I had so many questions that I needed answers to. I just did. She kind of pissed me off; I wanted to see her now, and not whenever she wanted to see me.

After work, I decided to stop by her apartment. I decided not to call her. I wanted to see why she had to wait to see me. I knocked on her door.

"Who is it?" She yelled.

"It's me, Hassan."

She opened the door and stood there, staring me down.

"You not goin' invite me in?"

"I thought I told you that I would get back to you?" she screwed her face up at me.

"Imani, come on bae. I just need to see you. I miss you, yo."

I looked back to make sure no one was around. I was a G and I couldn't risk anyone hearing me beg a female.

"Come on, this is me. I just want to talk," I pleaded.

"Man, come in, but the minute you start any kind of shit, I'm putting you out."

I had no idea who she was checking like that. But I was a patient man who knew how to play his cards right. I didn't say a word. I stepped in and closed the door behind me.

Out of nowhere, Josiah walked from the back. "What this nigga doing here?"

"Watch your mouth, dude. This your mom's crib and she invited me. You got that, young nigga?"

"Hassan, shut up. Josiah, I just want to talk to him."

"You the grown up, you 'ont have to explain shit to him."
This nigga was beginning to become a nuisance.

"You invited him here after what he did to you? You
dumber than I thought." He hissed his teeth and walked
out the door.

"What's his problem? You need to get him in check, the
little nigga getting out of control.

"Really, Hassan? And you don't think you had anything
to do with it?"

"Babe, listen, you right I have a lot to do with it. I know
I fucked up, Imani."

"Fucked up? You caused me to lose my baby. That's
more than fucking up."

"I agree and I'm sorry for e'erything that I put you
through. I swear, Imani, I snapped after what that nigga
Corey said about Josiah being his son. I was crushed, B.
Fuck, I'm still hurting. Do you get that?"

I know I can pull this off, I assured myself. I blinked a
few times and eventually I got a few teardrops. That was
enough to get myself crying. This wasn't anything new; I
learned early on women were suckers for a nigga crying.
Let's see how good I really am. It didn't take long for her
to fall for the foolery. In no time, she was professing her
love for me. I really missed fucking her, so I made up
by tearing that pussy up right in the middle of the living
room. She wasn't too worried about her son walking in
on us and I definitely didn't give a fuck about him. If you
asked me, I would have loved for him to see me burning
his mama's ass up. Maybe then he'd learn to shut the fuck
up.

After having sex, I knew I had her where I wanted her.
"Sit down, B, lemme rap wit' you. Yo, how long you and
Corey been fucking around?"

"I thought you let that go. What was all that crying and you telling me you love me? Was all that a lie to get some pussy?"

"Imani, chill out. You of all people should know I ain't hard up for pussy. Now answer my question. In order for us to move on, I need to know the truth. You understand?" I looked her in the eyes.

Before she could respond, her son walked in. The tension was on the rise and I felt like it would only get worse. I decided it was best for me to bounce.

"Yo, B. We will finish this at a different time. I'm out." I got up, unlocked the door and walked out.

I was furious that I didn't get the answers that I needed. I pulled out my phone to hit up Big Dre. His phone went directly to voicemail. I was careful not to leave any messages. I let out a long sigh. *What's next?* I thought.

CHAPTER TWENTY-NINE

Imani Gibson

Hassan had been weighing on my mind heavily. I was angry with him; I didn't understand why he had to bring our business to his mama and them. My son was the innocent party in all of this chaos and they were the only family he knew. God, Hassan made my ass itch, but I still loved him.

I know I was being a fool, but when he called, my heart skipped a few beats. I played it off, like I didn't want to see him. To say I was surprised when he knocked on my door was an understatement.

I was happy to see him; there was something about this man that triggered some sort of excitement whenever he got close to me. I wanted to tell him about e'erything that I'd been through. I wanted to lay in his arms and have him tell me everything was gonna be all right. That wasn't going to happen though. I still felt anger toward him for all the shit he put me through, from burning my pussy to cheating and beating on me, which resulted in me losing my child.

I admit, as strong as my mind was my heart was still weak for him. I felt bad for him when he started to cry; I'd never seen Hassan in a fragile state before. It hurt my heart to see him hurting like that, and if I didn't know before, I knew now that his love for me was genuine. He started kissing on me and I quickly fell for it. My pussy tongue was thumping and my drawers were getting wet. I wanted him inside of me bad. I knew if I put it on him, I could get him back where I wanted him. So I did just that: I sucked his dick and threw this pussy back on him. I kept looking at the door because I was scared that Josiah might bust in. The last thing I needed was for my son to see me getting fucked. *Lord, let him hurry up*, I thought as I threw my pussy on him.

I thought after we had sex the drama would end, but the nigga surprised me and started to ask me a million and one questions. Fuck, I was not trying to go there with him, I already got my ass whooped by this shit and I'd be damned if I was going to take another beating for the same shit.

I was happy when Josiah bust in the door. That angered Hassan a little and he stormed out the door. Even though I didn't want him to leave, I welcomed him leaving then because I didn't want my answers to trigger him in any way. God knew I was tired of being a damn punching bag. A bitch like me deserved better. I jumped in the shower and while I washed up my mind ran to Destiny. As much as I hated that bitch for the shit she did to me and for coming between Hassan and me, I think she was my only chance to get some good money so I could get me and my son out of all this bullshit.

Earlier when Hassan was fucking me, I was so close to confessing everything to him. I wanted to let him know that his precious wife had some shit up her sleeve, but something inside convinced me not to do that. The thing was, Hassan knew Josiah was not his seed, so that meaned my money was cut off and I was dead-ass broke. So my decision was pretty simple.

After I got out the shower, I picked up the phone and dialed her number.

"Hello," she answered.

"I know who it is. I take it you called me with good news?"

I rolled my eyes and took a deep breath. I hated the sound of this bitch's voice, but a boss bitch will do what she has to do until she can do better.

"Yeah, well, you 'ont leave me with much of a choice," I replied sarcastically.

"We need to meet tomorrow and we can discuss what I need from you. We can meet over at Cross County. There're a few restaurants over there. We can have lunch. Please be careful. Not sure if you're still talking to Hassan, but he's smarter than you think. Twelve p.m. is good for me. Call me when you're leaving out."

"Nah, I ain't talk to him and I'll be there." I hung up.

This ho thought she was slick with her comment about Hassan. That was a low-key way of trying to find out if Hassan and I have been talking. Her ass should've known I wasn't a fool; I would never let her know what I was doing with my man.

Destiny Clarke

I thought about what Mama said about getting a gun. I wasn't a killer and I didn't want to be one, but I was at a point where I didn't trust Hassan and things were getting sticky between us.

I googled gun stores and a few popped up. I picked the one closest to the house. I got up and got dressed in a pair of Levi's jeans and a nice blouse. The weather was changing; spring was definitely in the air. I could finally show off my little petite shape. After I got dressed, I put on a pair of Michael Kors sandals and grabbed my purse and walked out into the fresh air. I didn't know what it was, but I was feeling myself, both physically and mentally.

I parked in the space that was available and walked into the store. I was kind of nervous because I didn't like guns, but then again, I didn't like a lot of things, but I had to live with them.

"Good morning. Welcome to Olinville Arms, how may I help you?" A voice startled me.

I stopped dead in my tracks and turned back toward the door. I didn't belong here. *I should leave,* I thought.

"Were you interested in looking at our firearms?"

"Good morning." I turned around to face the tall, stalky Indian man. "Uh, oh yes, please." I nervously said.

"Do you have an idea of what you want? We carry all different makes and models."

"No, I just need something small."

I walked over to the counter. There were a bunch of cute little guns in the display counter.

Instantly, a picture of me shooting Hassan popped into my head. It wasn't a great image, but it gave me life.

"Umm, what about this one?" I pointed to a green gun."

"Yes sure, that's the Nighthawk Lady Hawk. It's a pretty decent firearm for ladies."

He took it out, and handed it to me. "Hold it."

I took, and rubbed my hand all over it.

"How can I get this?"

"Have you ever owned a gun?"

"No."

"Well, you will need to fill out the gun permit form for the state of New York. It usually takes six to eight months to get processed."

"What, you mean, I'll have to wait all that time? This is pure bullshit."

"Yes, I'm sorry. That's the law." He smiled at him.

I handed the gun back to him, "Thank you. Have a nice day."

I turned and walked out of the shop. I was disappointed to know I couldn't get the gun. "Six to eight months, shit Hassan might've killed my ass by then," I mumbled under my breath.

I got into my car and cut it on. I noticed it was 11:25 a.m. *Imani hasn't called yet,* I thought. I hope that old trifling-ass whore didn't change her mind. Soon as the thought left my mind, my phone started ringing.

"Hello, where you want to meet?"

"Let's meet at the Red Lobster in the Cross County shopping center. It's on Xavier Dr. You might want to google it."

"I know where it's at. I'm on the way."

I tried to muster every bit of energy inside of me in order to deal with this whore. I couldn't stand to be around her, but I knew there was no other way. I put my shades on and pulled off.

CHAPTER THIRTY

Hassan Clarke

Ever since Imani and I fell out, I'd been hanging with Tanya more. She was cool in the beginning, but the more time I spent with her, the clingier she became. It got worse after she invited me home to meet her parents. I probably shouldn't have done that, but the way she was fucking and sucking me, how could I refuse? It was the weekend and I had decided to get a room at the Ramada Inn on Baychester Avenue. After eating her pussy for a good thirty minutes, I finally put the dick on her, real good. After I came, I lay back on the bed, trying to catch my breath. That young pussy drained a nigga. I found myself having to drink a few bottles of Monster right before we fucked. I couldn't let her feel like she was giving me a run for my money.

"I need to talk to you." She rolled over to be closer beside me.

"What's up? Talk to me." I put one arm around her.

"Umm. . ." She paused.

"What's up babe?" I turned her face toward me.

"I'm pregnant."

"You w-what?" I stuttered.

I looked at her hoping to get a quick "I'm joking," but instead she had tears rolling down her face.

That made it hard for me. I didn't know how to respond. I wanted to scream at her dumb ass—now wasn't the time for her to be talking 'bout no damn baby. Shit, if Destiny got wind of this, my ass was going to be roasted in court.

"I'm scared. My period was late and I went to my doctor and he confirmed it."

"I thought you were on birth control. How did you manage to get pregnant?" I yelled.

"You're acting like you're not happy. You love me and I love you and now we can finally be together."

I sat there, staring. This young bitch was dumber than I originally thought. *I don't fucking love you,* I thought.

"Listen, B. I do love you, but I'm about to get a divorce. You're a law student, so you know how that is. The last thing I need is for Destiny's lawyers to find out that I got a child on the way. That can't happen. You hear me," I yelled.

"What are you saying? I don't understand. Are you saying you don't want our child?" she cried.

Oh man, another emotional bitch, I thought.

"Nah, babe, that's not what I'm saying at all. What I'm saying is, if you have an abortion, after the divorce, I can get you pregnant again and we can be a family then." I smiled and touched her face.

"Hassan, I'm far from one of these dumb females out here. I am not killing my child. So you need to decide who you are going to be with, just know that, whatever you decide, it better include my child in it."

"Bitch, you threatening me?" I shoved her away from me.

I thought about killing that bitch and her fucking seed, but I knew that wouldn't be a good move. The bitch was white and I know her people wouldn't cease until they find her ass.

"Yo, get your shit and get out of my room. You can call me when you get some sense."

She didn't say a word. She got up, smiled at me, and walked into the bathroom.

"What the fuck," I yelled out. Man, e'erytime I turned around, one of these hoes was having an issue. Fuck, this dick got me in more trouble than any other motherfucking thing. Shit, it was a blessing and a curse at the same damn time.

I watched as that bitch gathered her things and walked out, slamming the door behind her. I shook my head in disgust. I got up and poured me a cup of Hennessy Black. I needed something strong to drown out this latest news. I grabbed the remote and cut on the TV.

"Breaking news: The police are confirming that thirty-eight-year-old Corey Blackman was shot outside of his apartment building. According to the police, a lone gunman walked up to the victim and fired multiple gunshots. He then walked off and disappeared into thin air. According to the police, the victim is in critical condition at Lady of Mercy Hospital," the TV reporter said.

I took a big gulp, hurried to the table, and poured another cup. I grabbed my cell phone to call this nigga, but quickly decided against it. I am a defense attorney, and I knew about that cell phone record.

"Fucking idiot. He was supposed to make sure that nigga was dead." I shook my head.

I couldn't sit still. I kept pacing back and forth. God, I hoped this fool didn't leave any evidence. There was no way I was going to prison for some fucked ass shit this fuck nigga did.

CHAPTER THIRTY-ONE

Destiny Clarke

As I sat across from that whore, I couldn't help but notice that she was nothing special. I stared at her, trying to see something that my husband might've seen in her. There was nothing. She was a broke, loud-mouthed bitch. I was pretty sure she could fuck and suck cock real well. Other than that, I really didn't see what else she had to offer.

After talking with Imani and letting her know what I wanted, she decided to videotape herself and Hassan having sex. I still was kind of leery of her because I knew she was still in love with him and she wanted him in her life. The only thing I was counting on was her love for money and I knew her greedy ass wasn't going to give up a chance to get fifty grand.

We parted ways as I headed to my lawyer's office. I wanted to give him an update on what'd been going on and to let him know I was ready to file the divorce papers.

"Hello Mrs. Clarke. Attorney Wallock is waiting for you."

"Good afternoon. Thank you."

I walked off and knocked, then pushed open the door to the plush office. *There must be plenty divorces going around, 'cause he is eating good,* I thought.

"Mrs. Clarke, how are you doing today?" he stood up and shook my hand.

"Actually, today is a good day for me."

"Please sit down."

We sat down discussing everything that the forensic accountant found out about Hassan's finances. That dirty bastard was hiding money in different places, even in the Cayman Islands. I just sat there, listening to all the dirt they dug up on him.

"I say we have a pretty good case against him. I can get you alimony and half of everything he acquired during the marriage."

Shit, that was pretty much everything. *The nigga was broke when I met him*, I thought.

"One more thing: I need to file for full custody of my daughter."

"All right. Custody cases are different and will be handled in juvenile and family courts."

"All right, let's do the divorce first. I want this bastard out of my life," I spoke with conviction.

I sat there and watched him as he wrote down information.

"Okay, I have everything here. Based on all the information that you gave me and all the evidence against your husband, we can file for a fault-based divorce for any of these reasons: Cruel and Inhuman Treatment, and under New York State law, you are qualified because of the way he treats you. If you went through any kind of verbal and physical abuse, we can include that in our case. We will need evidence to support this claim and I will also include adultery as a reason for the divorce. This can be easily proven by the pictures that were taken, him buying his mistress that Lexus, and whatever other evidence we have when we walk into court. He is a lawyer, so he knows the law. We want to be prepared."

"Got you. I'm more than ready to get the ball rolling. Well, I'll be in touch soon." I got up, shook his hand and walked out.

I was pretty confident that we had a great case against him. The bastard had no idea what he was up against. He fucked with the wrong woman.

I had to pick Amaiya up from school and I got there just in time. I watched as my baby stood by the sidewalk talking to a boy. I honked the horn to let her know I was there.

I watched as she gave the boy a hug and walked to the car.

"Hey Ma," she said, leaning over to give me a kiss.

"Hey babe. So who was that boy?"

"A friend, Ma."

"A friend? Do you hug all your friends like that?" I looked at her and smiled.

"Ma, chill out. Jamal is only a friend."

"Ok, can I ask you a question?"

"Oh God, here we go. No, Ma, I'm not having sex and no, I don't have a boyfriend."

"Ok, just checking."

"I know, Ma. You want me to finish high school and go to college. You want me to get married before sex, all that."

"No, I understand you're growing up into a beautiful young woman. I just feel like you shouldn't rush to be in a relationship. Take your time and the right boy will come along."

"Ma, does this have anything to do with the fact, that you and daddy are getting a divorce? "

"Not really, just don't want you to make the same mistakes that I did. That's all." I reached over and rubbed her hand.

I wished I could protect her for the rest of her life, but I knew I couldn't. I just prayed she would never have to experience any of the shit that I'd been through, 'cause God knews these niggas weren't worth a damn.

I cooked Salisbury steak and mashed potatoes for dinner for Amaiya and myself. I had to get used to it just being the two of us again. I never thought that my marriage would've come to this, but it did. Tears welled up in my eyes as I sat there reminiscing on the great times we had. I remembered our first date; the first time he touched me. It was magic. I had no understanding of how we went from sugar to shit.

After my baby girl got in bed, I cleaned up the kitchen, cut the lights off, and walked upstairs. I felt a slight headache coming on, so I took two Tylenol and got into the shower. I soaked in the tub for a good twenty-five minutes then got out. I stood in front of the mirror to dry myself off. I glanced at myself and ran my hand across my breast. Oh, how I missed a man touching me. I longed for the closeness of a man, but I'd be damned if I was just going to be out there fucking. Now that this bum done gave me herpes, I had no idea what kind of sex life I was going to have. I quickly got dressed and got into my bed. The thought of having an STD that couldn't be cured was very depressing.

Tears started to flow again. I tried my entire life not to fuck every nigga that came my way. Shit, I could count on my fingers all the niggas that ran up in me, all because I didn't want to be a whore or end up with a fucking disease. What good did it do me? None, 'cause this pussy-ass nigga done burned my ass for good.

I must've fallen asleep because I felt someone shaking me. I opened my eyes. I thought it was Amaiya, but hell no, it was this bum, laying butt-ass naked beside me.

"What the hell you think you doing?"

"I'm trying to make love to my wife. Is that a problem?"

"Don't fucking touch me," I yelled and slapped his fucking hand away.

I jumped up, and tried to run out of the room, but he jumped in front of me and blocked me in.

"Move out of my fucking way, Hassan. I swear to God if you touch me. . . " I stepped toward him.

"W-h-a-t you goin' do?" he slurred his words.

His breath was stinking with alcohol and he could barely stand still. I figured this fool was drunk.

I tried to push him out of my way, but even in his drunken state, I was no match for him.

He raised his hand and slapped me in my face. I tried to slap him back, but he grabbed my arm and threw me on the bed and got on top of me. I wanted to scream, but my baby was in the other room and I didn't want her to hear any of this nonsense.

"Hassan, stop get up off me," I screamed.

"Nah bitch, shut up. This pussy is mine and I want to fuck." He pried my legs open.

Emotions stirred up in me. I had a flashback to when my Daddy used to fuck me. Tears started to roll down my face. My body tensed up and I whispered a prayer to God.

"God, please help me. I can't go through this again."

"What the fuck you say bitch?"

I realized then he wasn't going to stop and this bastard was really going to rape me. I swallowed hard, wiped my tears, and then spoke.

"Hey babe, you ain't got to do all that. I've missed you fucking me," I lied through clenched teeth.

That caught his attention 'cause he looked at me and smiled.

"Really? You miss me babe?" He grinned.

"Of course. I miss sucking your cock. Matter of fact, let me show you how much I miss you." I smiled at him.

He eased up off me and lay on his back. I got on my knees and took his erected cock into my hands and licked the tip. I glanced at him as he was smiling. I took the full length in and he groaned hard. I looked at him and he was smiling with his eyes closed.

I used every bit of strength in me and sunk my teeth down on his cock while holding it in place.

"*Aarghhhhhhhhhhhhh*! You stupid bitch, I'm going to kill you," he said as he grabbed my neck.

I couldn't breathe as I tried to bite harder, but that made him squeeze harder. I had no choice but to let go and gasp for air. I then bit down on his hand again so he could let go of my neck, which he did.

I jumped up and ran out the room as fast as I could and into Amaiya's room while he yelled and called me all kind of bitches.

"Bitch, where the fuck you at? I swear I'm goin' kill yo ass." He yelled down the hallway.

I locked Amaiya's bedroom door.

"What's wrong, Mama? Why is daddy yelling?" She jumped out of her sleep.

"Baby, just lie back down." I tried to comfort her.

I couldn't believe this fool tried me like that. I wish I could've bitten his cock off clean; that way, he wouldn't be able to fuck another bitch in his life. I was scared to go out the door, so I sat in the corner in my daughter's room. I was hurt and feeling broken—this nigga done stirred up old emotions inside of me; emotions that I had buried deep down inside of myself.

Imani Gibson

I was helping her and he was going to whoop my ass. There was no way I was going to risk getting another beat down because of this bitch. Destiny bought me a camcorder. It was little, but I could tell it was an expensive piece of equipment. I wanted to laugh because that bitch had no problem spending all that money just so she could get a recording of Hassan and I having sex when he came over. I had to put it in a spot where it wouldn't be visible, and I'd keep it off until it was show time. Things were not going good for me at all. I used the money that Destiny gave me to pay some bills; I was behind on everything because Hassan used to pay the bills, but he had not given me a dollar since he found out that Corey was Josiah's daddy. That was fucked up on Hassan's behalf because he left me and my son for dead, even though he claimed he loved me. There was no way I was going back to being broke and Hassan was going to wish he had continued throwing me a few stacks.

Josiah wouldn't ease up on his questioning about who his dad was. Apparently Charmaine's trifling ass called him to tell him that she was not his auntie. That bitch knew she was wrong for doing that. They couldn't hurt me, so they hurt the person closest to me, my son.

"Ma, we need to talk seriously. I asked you before and you blew me off. If Dad ain't my Daddy, then who is?" he asked in a serious tone.

"Baby, I told you before, Hassan is your daddy. They just starting some bullshit and because they can't get to me, they trying to use you," I lied.

I swear I couldn't bring myself to tell my son the truth.

"Ma, I know you lying to me. It's sad. You teach me to not lie, but here I am asking you a very important question and you keep lying to my face." He gritted on me.

What did this little boy want me to tell him? That his mama was a whore and wasn't sure who his daddy was? How could I admit that shit to him?

"Baby. . ." I took a deep breath then continued.

"Listen, Josiah: I love you and that's all that really matters. Baby, you 'ont need no daddy." I tried to hug him.

"But I do, Ma. I want one. I need to know who my Daddy is. I 'ont want to be one of these niggas out here that don't know their father."

I took his hand in mine. Tears welled up in my eyes. I looked into my son's eyes then spoke:"Hassan is right. He's not your daddy." I regretted those words as soon as they parted my lips.

He snatched his hand away from me and stood up. "You been lying to me my whole life. Had me calling this man dad, and he wasn't. Why would you do that, Ma? Why?" he yelled.

"Calm your voice. I'm sorry, Josiah. I did not know. Baby, I swear I didn't know." I cried.

"So who is my father? Do you even know?"

I swallowed hard. I didn't want to tell him that that bum was his daddy, but I saw he was dead serious.

"This guy named Corey is your father." I sniffed.

"That's the same dude, Dad or Hassan, I don't even know what to call him anymore, was talking about. You knew he was telling the truth all along."

"Josiah, I'm sorry. It was a mistake, baby."

"A mistake? You've been lying to me for all these years and now you're telling me it was a mistake. I trusted you, Ma, but my whole life has been a lie. I hate you. I swear I fucking hate you." He said, opening the door and dashing out.

"Josiah," I ran to the door and yelled.

He ran fast down the stairs. I wanted to run after him, but instead I ran back inside and flopped down on the couch, crying.

"No God, that's my baby boy. I'm sorry that I lied to him. I'm sorry." I cried.

Any other time, I would say it was going to be all right. But not this time. I knew my child was hurting because of the fucked up decision that I made. I'd lost everything and I couldn't afford to lose him too. I got up to pour me a glass of wine. I needed to drown out the pain that was burning my insides.

What else could go wrong? I thought before I took a big gulp.

Hassan Clarke

I walked around on pins and needles for days. Every time I saw a police officer while I was driving I kept thinking they were coming for me. I hadn't heard from that nigga, Dre, and I was too scared to call him in case the police were on to him. I couldn't believe the nigga fucked up like that. He was supposed to be a certified killer. I shook my head in disbelief.

I stayed glued to the television whenever I was not at work. I wanted to know if the police had any suspects or witnesses. I started drinking heavily; life was weighing on me. I had one crazy bitch that was trying to put me out of my house, another put a bastard on me that wasn't even mine, and then one bitch talking 'bout how she was pregnant and now this nigga done fucked up. Fuck my life. There wasn't shit else that could possibly go wrong. I got a big bottle of Hennessy Black and opened it up, even though I was driving. I was in despair. I wished I had someone to talk to. Shit, I wasn't going to lie; I missed talking to Imani. She used to be my rock when I was going through shit. I thought 'bout popping up over there, but decided not to. Her motherfucking son was blowing me and I didn't have the strength to fuck his little ass up tonight. I decided to take my ass home. I didn't give a fuck if Destiny's bitch ass didn't want me there. Fuck that bitch. Matter of fact, I was goin' fuck that bitch tonight.

I opened the door and walked up the stairs. The house was quiet, so either she wasn't home or she was asleep. I walked into the room and quickly noticed she was asleep. I stood there, looking at her. She looked so peaceful. I quickly took off my clothes and got into the bed with her. I started to rub on her shoulder. It didn't take long for the bitch to wake up and start snapping. This trick needed to be taught a lesson. I was her motherfucking husband and that pussy belonged to me. Her deranged ass started fighting me, but I wasn't going to give up. I was going to take what was rightfully mine.

The bitch tried to run out of the room, but she wasn't going anywhere—not before I got the pussy. My daddy once told me that when a bitch acting like she 'ont want the dick, it really meant that she was begging me to give it to her. Her arrogance only made me angrier and I was determined to fuck her hard, fuck her in her ass raw.

She tried to slap me, but even in my tipsy state, I was quick to block it. I snapped and grabbed her by the neck and threw her on the bed. I really wanted to choke the life out of that bitch. I would definitely get pleasure out of seeing that bitch in a casket. Then I wouldn't have to worry about giving her a dime in the divorce.

I don't know what happened, but that bitch must've gotten the memo that I wasn't going to cease until I got the pussy. She decided to give me some head, and even though there was nothing special 'bout her head game, it would do right about now because I was tipsy and horny. The minute her mouth touched my dick it sent electric volts through my body. I closed my eyes, savoring the moment, and because I was too caught up in the sensation I was getting from her.

"*Aaarghhhhhhhhh*," I screamed out. This dumb bitch sank her teeth down on my dick.

"Stupid bitch. I'm going to kill you." I wrapped my hands around her neck; my intention was to break that shit off her body.

The pain was unbearable; I had to tighten my grip so she knew it was not a game. The bitch finally let my dick go as I continued to squeeze until that ho bit my hand. I let go, but before I could grab that bitch again, she ran out the room. I got up and stumbled to the bathroom. I cut the lights on to examine my dick. I peeped the imprint of her teeth, but luckily for her ass, there was no blood. I got a warm rag and applied pressure to my dick.

I didn't chase after that bitch. By now I was no longer tipsy and was in my right frame of mind. I quickly got dressed and left the house. I called Imani's phone.

"Hello," she answered groggily.

"Yo, what's good with you? Why you sound like you crying, you good?"

"Nah, I'm fine. What do you want?"

"I want to see you."

"You know where I'm at."

"I'm on the way."

On my way over there, all I could think about was my hatred for Destiny. Tomorrow, I would file for a divorce. I didn't care how much money that bitch thought she would get. She could have all that little chump change in our joint account and I'd pay alimony. There was no reason to keep that good for nothing bitch around.

I banged on the door. It was late and these niggas were robbing people and I didn't want to become one of their victims. I had to make sure I got a burner; after all, I was a defense attorney and I needed protection.

"Hey babe, "I walked in.

"Hey."

"I'm tired as shit. I need to lie down." I walked to the
room.

"Aiight, lie down."

It was strange that she didn't try to argue. Instead, she
got into the bed beside me and tried to rub my back. My
dick got hard instantly, which made it hurt. Even though
I wanted to fuck her, my shit was sore and swollen.
There was no way I could even attempt to stick my dick
anywhere. I closed my eyes, pretending like I was asleep.

I was tired, mentally and physically. I needed a break
from everything in my life, including all these bitches. I
swear, I needed some new hoes.

CHAPTER THIRTY-TWO

Imani Gibson

Hassan spent the night for the first time in a long time. Any other time, I would've asked why he wasn't at home with his wife, but this time was different. I was on a mission to get evidence of him sleeping around on his wife. I thought when he got here he would want to fuck, but he surprised me by telling me he was tired and wanted to lay down. Things seemed different. I tried to rub on him, hinting that I wanted to fuck, but he didn't budge. He lay there until he fell asleep. *This is strange*, I thought before I dozed off.

The next morning, I awoke to Hassan kissing all over me. I didn't resist. Even though I was on a mission, I still loved to feel his touch. He still had control over my body, mind, and soul. He kissed my neck, and then slowly made his way down to my stomach. He massaged my clit and then inserted his finger into my moist pussy.

"*Aweee*," I groaned out in ecstasy.

His touch sent electric volts through my entire body.

"Daddy, I want you. Please," I begged for the dick.

"Relax, I got you." His head made its way between my legs.

I bit down on my lip as he sucked on my clit. I tried my best not to scream because I knew Josiah was in his room.

"Hmmm. . . Daddy, please fuck me," I whispered in his ear.

I wasn't worried about anything that was being recorded. I was all for myself and my guilty pleasures.

He ate me out, and I came in his mouth. He slurped up every drop, and then got on top of me. He stuck his dick all the way in, and started long-stroking me. Even though it was touching my soul, I welcomed every inch of his manhood.

"Oh, oh, I love you, Hassan. I love you, fuck me harder," I mumbled.

"I got you babe." He went deeper, breaking my walls down.

"*Owiee.*" I moaned.

He stabbed harder as I threw the pussy on him. I really missed this. I miss our souls connecting as one. I felt his dick harden as he grabbed my butt, and pulled me closer to him.

"*Aargh,*" he groaned loudly.

"Shhh." I put my hand over his mouth to muffle the sounds.

He pulled out, and bust all over my chest. I saw he was being careful. I guess he didn't want a child with me, after all.

I lay there for a few minutes. I watched as he got up, put on his boxers, and walked out of the room. I closed my eyes and smiled to myself. My pussy was sore from him pounding my walls. I knew he missed fucking me and I missed having him in my life.

He walked back into the room, and sat at the edge at the bed.

"Hey babe, you all right?"

"Yeah, I'm good. Just thinking about how good that pussy is."

I sat up and scooted closer to him. "Really, hm. . .Let me find out you pussy whipped," I joked.

"Chill out, B. You know a nigga checking for you, but I just can't get over the shit you did to me. It still hurts deep down that Josiah ain't my seed. I just want to know what the fuck did I do to deserve this? Even though, I was out here messing wit' these other bitches, you always had my heart. You know that."

I felt bad that I had put him through this. I wished I could change everything, but it wasn't possible. I rubbed his shoulder. "Hassan, I am so sorry. I swear to you, I only messed wit' that boy one time and it was because we both was drinking," I cried.

"Imani, this ain't 'bout you fucking the nigga. You lied and said that Josiah was my seed. I gave you money for him. I provided for y'all. I feel like a fucking fool. I'm embarrassed to go 'round the people I know 'cause I know they laughing about this shit."

"Hassan, fuck what e'erybody saying. This is me and you. I felt embarrassed when you went and married that ho, but I still stayed with you. Why can't you forgive me so we can move on?"

"Yo, B, it ain't that easy. I'm a man with pride. My name carries weight in this state."

This nigga was pissing me off. He was more worried about how people would look at him instead of worrying about me.

"Hassan, this is us, boo. I'm patiently waiting on you to divorce Destiny."

"Fuck that bitch. She's dead to me. I don't ever want to hear you mention her name," he yelled.

"Damn, calm down. I didn't mean to upset you."

"I'm sorry. I ain't mean to yell at you. It's just the mention of that bitch's name drives me crazy. Nobody understands what I go through with her ass."

Listening to him, I kind of felt bad for him. I thought about telling him about the plan that Destiny came up with. I swear I didn't want to help that bitch bring him down.

"Hassan, I'm going to need some money to pay these bills."

"What? You better call that nigga Corey. That nigga was popping all that shit 'bout taking care of you and his seed," he lashed out.

"Really, you know damn well Corey don't have no money."

"Ha, ha, so your dumb ass went and fucked a nigga that's broke, had a baby by him, and now you want little old me to take care of you and that little bastard. Nah B, I love you and all, but you goin' have to find you another fool."

I sat there, looking at this nigga spit venom at me. A few seconds ago, I almost confessed some shit to him but I was happy that I kept my mouth shut because this confirmed that, he was not trying to be with me. I was good for fucking, but not to pay these fucking bills.

"Get out of my house!" I yelled.

"What you say to me?" he got up and stared me down.

I stood up and stared back at him. "You heard me. I said get out of my house. I'm tired of the way you treat me. You know I love you, but I'm tired. You've been slinging that dick all over this motherfucking city, and I forgave you. But you act like the shit I did is the fucking worst."

He raised his hand and slapped me twice, back to back.

"Bitch, don't you ever talk to me like that. You're a fucking ho. I made you somebody."

I held my face, which was still burning from the slap. I decided that I wasn't going to cry, at least not in front of him.

"I fucking hate you. Now get out of my shit before I call the police to put you out." I opened the door.

"Bitch, fuck you, do you know who I am? I'm Hassan Clarke, the defense attorney."

He lunged toward me, grabbed my neck and started to choke me. I tried to scream, but he applied more pressure. He punched me, nonstop in my face, until blood started to spew out. I started to lose consciousness. All I could think about was this being my last time on this earth. . . .

I woke up in the hospital. I could barely open my eyes, but when I forced them open I noticed two uniformed policemen standing over my bed. I knew the hospital must have called them.

"Ms. Gibson, I'm Officer Maxwell and this is Sergeant Oliver. We're here to a take a report and possibly file charges on whoever did this to you."

Shit just got real, I thought. Hassan had always put his hands on me, but has never gone this far. This time, he bloodied my face and broke my nose.

I closed my eyes, which were hurting from opening them up.

"Ms. Gibson, can you tell us, who did this to you?"

I hesitated, then I spoke, "Hassan Clarke."

"Hassan Clarke? That name sounds familiar," Sergeant Oliver said.

Oh here we go, these fools knew him. He had always bragged about how he was tight with some of the officers in the Bronx.

"I got it. Are you talking about the popular defense attorney Hassan Clarke?"

I hung my head down, "Yes," I mumbled.

"Well, tell us what happened."

I looked at both of them. They didn't seem too interested after I told them who did this to me. I didn't give a fuck. I was tired of covering for a nigga that didn't give a fuck about me.

Destiny Clarke

After last night, I was more determined then ever to get Hassan out of my house. The nigga had been seconds away from raping me, so I knew the next time I might not be as lucky.

After Amaiya left for school, I went on a rampage. I went through his closet in the spare bedroom, grabbed all his expensive suits and leather, foreign-made shoes. I made several trips inside to make sure I had everything. I got two big bottles of bleach that I had in the basement, put everything in the back yard, and went on a rampage. I emptied the bottles onto everything he owned.

I was no longer hurting. I was filled with rage. I'd had enough of this bastard playing me and disrespecting me. He had definitely violated me when he tried to take pussy that didn't belong to him anymore.

I then grabbed some big trash bags and threw the soiled clothing and shoes into the bags. I took them and dropped them off on the curb. I saw my nosy next-door neighbor outside raking his yard. He looked at me strangely as I pulled the bags to the curb. I smiled at him, turned, and walked back inside.

I searched through my CD's and found my old Waiting to Exhale soundtrack.

"While all the time that I was loving you, you were busy loving yourself. I would stop breathing if you told me to, now you're busy loving someone else, eleven years out of my life, besides the kids, I have nothing to show Wasted my years a fool of a wife. I should have left your ass long time ago," Mary J. Blige's voice echoed through my Bose surround system.

I went through the house and one by one, I broke all the pictures that we had taken together. Our wedding pictures included. There was shattered glass every-where, the exact way my heart was shattered. I kneeled down on my living room floor and I cried my heart out. I cried until there was nothing else in me. No more tears or any other emotions. I felt drained, so instead of cleaning up the mess I made, I decided to take a shower.

I didn't feel like driving, so I called Mama and asked her to pick up Amaiya from cheerleading practice. I guess I had dozed off because I was woken up by the phone ringing. I ignored it the first time, but it rang a second time. I got it off the dresser and looked, to see who was calling. It was the handsome Mr. Private Investigator Spencer. I wondered what he wanted since our business dealings were over.

"Hello, good evening," I said in a seductive tone, but I quickly corrected myself.

"Hello Mrs. Clarke, or do you go by a different name?"

"No, I'm still married. Working on the divorce now," I chuckled.

"Oh, I see." he paused.

"Well, what can I do for you, Mr. Spencer?"

"Well, I wanted to invite you out for dinner and maybe we could catch a movie as well."

"Oh my, I feel honored, but I am not trying to see anyone. As you know, I'm trying to get out of one messed-up relationship."

"I understand that, but it would be good for you to get out and enjoy yourself a little."

"I don't want to sound rude or anything like that, but I don't think that's a good idea. Sorry."

"All right, but if you change your mind, don't hesitate to call."

I didn't say anything and hung up the phone. Oh Lord, his voice did something to me. I smiled to myself, and then the sound of the doorbell interrupted my thoughts.

I ran downstairs, and peeped out the hole. It was Mama and Amaiya. I opened the door for them.

"Hey Mama."

"Hey babe. Hey Ma, you coming in?"

"I'll come in for a few."

I closed the door behind them and we walked toward the living room. Fuck, I totally forgot the place was a mess from the havoc I created earlier.

"What happened in here? Did somebody lose their mind and break all your stuff?"

"No, nothing happened. I just had a moment. I forgot to clean up."

"I'm happy you're feeling a little better. I don't know what happened in here earlier, but you might want to clean it up."

"I got it."

We hung around for little, just talking about everyday things. Mama decided to leave.

"Are you and Amaiya safe over here? I told you before that y'all can stay with me 'til the divorce is final."

"Ma, I told you before: this is my house and I'm not leaving for shit. I'm going to stay here and make sure that bastard don't mess my shit up. I worked too hard to buy this and I will not walk away from it."

"I understand. I'm just worried that he is goin' to show his black ass. I want y'all safe and away from him."

I saw the worried look on Mama's face. I hated that she worried so much.

"Look, Mama, I'm a big girl, and you raised me to be tough. I've had my share of weakness, but that shit is over. I have to grow a backbone and put my big girl panties on." I rubbed her back.

"Aiight sugar. Remember, I'm a phone call away." She kissed me on the cheek and then walked out the door.

After Mama, left I made some soup for Amaiya and myself. She then went to her room, and I went to lie down. My mind was racing and all over the place. I was thinking of divorcing Hassan. Yes, finally I'd be able to breathe again.

Thoughts of taking Mr. Spencer up on his offer crossed my mind, which made my heart flutter and my palms became sweaty. *Oh hell no, this can't be happening*, I thought. I was in one fucked up relationship that broke and shattered my heart into tiny pieces. I didn't know if I'd ever want another man. Shit, I could definitely understand why women turned to other women for comfort. These men nowadays were full of shit.

I pulled up my blanket, closed my eyes. What was the possibility of me finding love again?

I woke up to the banging of my downstairs door. My first instinct was somebody was trying to break in. I jumped out of the bed and grabbed my robe and my cell phone. That was when I heard "Bronx Police. Open up the door."

The police? Lord, this bitch done reported me, was the first thought that entered my mind. My heart started racing as I walked down the stairs. I looked through the peephole and there were three officers posted outside. I took a long sigh and then opened the door.

"Yes, may I help you?" I nervously asked.

"Ma'am, we are looking for Hassan Clarke. Is he home?"

"Uh, I'm not sure. We are separated and I don't know when he's here or not."

"Is that his car?" he pointed to the side of the house.

I peeped around the corner, "Yes that's his car. Let me see if he's upstairs."

I turned around, walked back inside and went up the stairs. I walked to his room, tried his door, but it was locked. I banged on the door a few times.

"Ma, what's going on?" Amaiya stepped out of her room.

"Honey, the police are here looking for your dad. Go back in your room."

I banged on his door a few more times. He opened the door, barely dressed and cock hard as hell.

"What the fuck you want?"

"The police is at the door. They want to speak with you."

"The police? What the heck they want with me?"

"Why don't you bring yo' black ass down there and find out."

I walked away from him and went back downstairs. "He's coming, officers."

"Thank you, ma'am."

I stood there as he walked downstairs, pulling a hoody over his head.

"Officers, I'm attorney Hassan Clarke. My wife told me y'all want to talk with me." He stepped outside.

"Hassan Clarke, you're under arrest for assault and battery. You have the right to remain silent. And if you give up that right, anything and everything you say, will be used against you, in the court of law." The slim police officer continued to read him his rights while he placed the cuffs on him.

"What y'all doing to my Daddy?" Amaiya rushed outside.

"Please get back in the house, ma'am."

I grabbed Amaiya, and hugged her tight.

"What the hell am I being arrested for? Who did I supposedly assault?" he yelled.

He turned to look at me. I stared at him. I didn't feel any kind of emotion. All I knew was his ass done did some shit he didn't have no business doing. "Babe, call Leon and let him know they're locking me up on some bullshit. He'll handle everything."

I continued looking at him. Any other time I was that "bitch" or whatever words came to his mouth, but now his ass needs me I'm "babe."

"Come on," I dragged Amaiya inside the house.

"Why they lock him up?"

"I have no idea, baby. Only your daddy knows what he did."

All this damn drama early in the morning. I knew these nosey neighbors of mine were up, probably trying to figure out what was going on. They weren't the only one; my ass was also trying to find out. I knew I had to wait until they booked him, then I could call to hear what his charges were.

I looked at the time. It was a quarter to six. It didn't make sense to go back to sleep. After all this drama, I needed a strong cup of coffee to start my day.

Amaiya was visibly upset about her father getting locked up, which I totally understood. Even though he barely paid her any attention, she loved him. I knew things might have been a little hard on her, first with the divorce and now this.

"Ma, can I stay home today? I don't feel too good."

"You know what? This is your first time being home from school. So yes, you can."

I watched as she dragged herself back to her room. I walked into my room and flopped down onto the bed. *Lord, I want this all to end soon,* I thought.